PAH

By Orla Owen

2021
Lavender Publishing

LAVENDER PUBLISHING

PAH
By Orla Owen

Copyright ©2021 Orla Owen

Produced and published in 2021
by Lavender Publishing

ISBN: 978-1-9160366-2-8
eISBN: 978-1-9160366-3-5

Typeset in Charter 11pt by Blot Publishing
www.blot.co.uk

www.orlaowen.com

For my family, I, C & E.

Susan

The steps that led to the navy door were crappy and chipped. Cigarette butts lay on both sides of the white-washed walls that guarded them, having missed the dented silver buckets they were meant to be tossed into. When Alice raised her hand to knock, the door was opened by a dark haired girl in blue and white checked pyjamas.

"I'm looking for Susan. Susan Brown."

The girl frowned. "What does she look like?"

"Slim, brown hair, dark brown, brown eyes that are nearly black, pale skin, pretty, sort of."

"That could be loads of people."

"Harsh looking. She can be. As if she's angry all the time."

"I know who you mean. I'll show you where her room is." Pyjama girl shut the door behind them.

The corridor was gloomy even with the central lights on. The stairs were two metres wide, the bannister a sticky mahogany above the white painted balustrades. They reached the second floor.

"Here you go."

Pyjama girl waited even though what happened next wasn't her business. Alice knocked. She knocked again.

"She's not in," said a girl in a nurse's uniform, her white headpiece similar to a nun's habit. "She's still on shift, doesn't finish for another two hours."

"Is it alright if I wait?"

"Sure."

Alice sat cross legged on the floor with her back against the wall. The seam of her ankle pants rose to her mid calves. She shoved her brown leather bag into the diamond shaped gap between her thighs and the soles of her feet, toes painted bright pink like bubble gum.

The nurse put a key in her door to open it. Pyjama girl went back downstairs. Alice tried to ignore the sick feeling as she waited, waited, waited.

~

Susan saw her visitor curled up on the floor, in front of her door, meaning there was no way she could get into the room without waking her. She was too tired to walk the streets in the hope that the unwanted guest would leave. And she wouldn't. Even if she had to wait all night, Susan knew Alice was the stubborn sort who'd do that, who wouldn't let go of the problem.

She stood in front of her sister and as she said her name she kicked her in the arm, hard.

"Ow. Shit. Ow." Alice uncurled to sitting. "Christ. Why did you do that? That really hurt."

She rubbed her hand up and down the tender skin as if that would make it better.

"Go away," said Susan.

"No."

"Yes."

"No."

"You're to leave. You're not welcome."

"Nice to see you too."

"Go away."

"They've got a buyer for the house. If you let me in I can tell you how much you'll be getting."

~

Alice threw her bag on Susan's bed and sat on the edge of it, legs together, palms flat either side of her thighs. The regulation nurses' blanket was prickly on the bottom of her legs, a darker shade of green than the walls. A black metal lampshade was hanging from the only light fitting, off centre, closer to the window than the door. There was no clue as to the personality of the room's occupant who was standing in the corner, next to a bare dressing table, not even a speck of dust on top of it.

"I'd love a drink, thanks for asking."

Susan glared at her guest.

"Yes, it was a long journey but hey, I found you so that's good. I mean that's wonderful isn't it my oh so loving sister?"

Susan walked down the corridor to the kitchen where she poured Alice a glass of water, half from the hot tap, half from the cold. That'd show her. The sink was full of dishes that people were meant to wash themselves, not leave with fat hardened on the china. Furious with the rule breakers, the in your face sister sitting in her bedroom, Susan put the glass on the empty drainer, lifted out a plate covered in horses that she knew was Rachel Pewter's favourite and smashed it onto the floor. Followed by the blue tea cup that the girl with curly blond hair gripped as if it was an actual comfort and a plate with congealed egg on its edges. She didn't know who that one belonged to. She picked up the water and walked calmly back to her room.

"Here." She went back into her corner, arms behind her back, rocking slightly from balls to heels. "You didn't have to come. I gave you the address so you could post me a cheque, not so you'd visit. You don't need to be here."

Alice grimaced at the lukewarm drink and unable to see anywhere she could leave it without the risk of a water mark, rested the base of the glass on her thighs.

"I thought with it being just the two of us left we could keep in touch."

"No."

"Why not?"

"I don't see the point. It'd be a wasted effort."

"It might not be. Now they're gone it might be easier."

"After the costs, how much is there?"

"The police came, the day after the funeral. They wanted to go over some things, wondered why you weren't there."

Susan shrugged.

"I told them you couldn't bear to be in the house, it was too exhausting. And you had to come back for your work."

Susan's bent fingers failed to grip the wallpaper behind her back so instead her nails scraped back and forth over it.

"One of them was keen to know more about that, about you being a nurse. I lied and said you're only a student so don't have access to drugs, that everything's supervised really carefully. Doris was there. She said that's true enough, she'd been a nurse for thirty years and it was all such a tragedy. We think he believed us what with her being so well respected in the community, living next door to us since we were little and all." Alice waited for her sister to say thank you. That's what she'd have done, what any normal person would do, surely. "Sweet little Doris, always so kind. I think she knew you know, that it was a strange house. I think she knew but just didn't say anything or didn't know what to say. And why would she?" Susan pressed against the wall with her fingers so hard that a piece of plaster buckled. She kept pushing at the newly formed hole as if she could escape through it. "I told the police that Daddy was maudlin, that sometimes he took the pills that were meant for Mother, in secret. Their eyes perked up at that so I said lots of times actually but we never told anyone as it was too shameful. Then I said that they loved each other, couldn't live without each other, hence both going within a week of each other. That was a good one wasn't it? That was clever of me?"

The sound that came from Susan was like a hurt animal caught in a trap, angry at the pain, desperate to be free. Shocked at her outburst, she stared at the floor in order to get a grip on herself. After three deep breaths she looked up at her little sister.

"How much is there?"

"Really? That's it? No thank you? No nice one for sorting it all out Sis? Jesus." Alice put the glass on the floor and fumbled in her bag. "Un-bloody-believable. You take the mickey you know that." She pulled out a brown envelope. Susan snatched it and retreated. After opening it, her face fell. Terse and furious, she held up a slip of yellow paper.

"This can't be it. What about the money from the house? And there must have been a good insurance policy. He worked in insurance for God's sake."

Alice thought she saw the start of tears in her sister's eyes, like when they were little.

"It turns out the wines he drank were expensive and the bets he placed on the horses were large and all lost. Fifty dollars and forty eight cents was all that was in their joint account. And there was no life insurance. I guess he hadn't planned on dying so soon."

"He should have had insurance. And her, she should have worked. There should have been more money. What was the point of it all if this is it?"

She waved the piece of paper in the air.

"Did you do something? I wondered then thought you couldn't have. I nearly said—"

"Like what?"

"Nothing." Alice was ready to spring off the bed, her hand hooked round her bag that could thwack her sister if needs be. She wanted to know the answer to her worry but was too scared of its consequences to ask again. "I think it's sad that their lives are over already after a life of bitter frowns. I mean, where was the joy? Imagine choosing to be so miserable."

"Pah."

"I'll send you a cheque once the house is sold."

"The good it'll do me." Susan pushed herself forward from the wall. "You should go now."

"What?"

"You need to go."

"I just spent twelve hours on a bus getting here."

"That's not my problem."

"Come on Susan. They're dead. It's just us now. Can't we—"

Susan scooted across the room, gripped her little sister by the elbow and pulled her to standing. Her fingers pressed into the funny bone so hard that Alice was bent to the side in pain with no choice but to walk alongside her.

"Get off me."

"Don't come again because I won't be here. I've got a new job. I move at the weekend."

Susan pushed Alice out of the door and closed it. Alice banged on it with her fist.

"Susan." Bang. "Susan." Bang. "Susan." Bang. "Susan!"

A blond girl's head poked out from the next room. "Can you keep it down? I'm trying to sleep in here." She slammed the door shut.

Alice muttered to herself. "Christmas. Christmas and Easter. Birthdays. No, not those. None of them. Not her. That's it. That's it done then. I can do this. I'll be fine on my own, of course I will."

She banged the fist of her right hand against her thigh. Boom. Boom. Boom. Her friends had warned her not to expect a happy ending with one so cold. She'd always been a strange sister, all of them had thought it, how different she was to the smiling Alice. Was that true? Was Susan odd and if so, was she born like that or did her parents make her turn out that way? Was it their mother that caused the meanness? She'd definitely got meaner as she got older. Alice should let it be, let Susan be. She should let it rest like the police had done and even the Priest had said some things were for the best and their souls were at peace now, God love them. So Alice would leave it be too, escape the grip, head to where her friend Lucinda had moved. She'd written that there were lots of people like them there, like Alice. The part of town Lucinda lived in was cheap as chips as it wasn't near the beach, dotted with cafes full of singers, actors, artists. Lucinda was training in some meditative yoga thing. Her plan was to teach the rich ladies down by St Kilda's. There was lots of work to choose from and Alice would be okay, her friends would be her family, life would move on and it would be less complicated with her big sister as well as her parents no longer a part of it.

Except she needed an address to send the money to. Otherwise it would be sitting in a bank account forever, eating away at her. She couldn't keep Susan's share. It had to be equal, that's what was fair. Alice wrote the solicitor's address on the back of the envelope from the telephone bill that was in her bag and slipped it under Susan's door.

"Write to them for the money. I'm going now."

She listened for movement. She knelt on the floor and craned her neck to see under the gap under the door to check if the envelope had been picked up but no feet or hands appeared. She used the handle to help her get to standing. Two nurses passed her and smiled. She smiled back. That's what normal people did, they smiled at one another. It was Susan who was odd, not her. It had to be. She followed the chatting nurses down the stairs and they held the front door open for her. It was so bright outside, Alice had to put her hand over her eyes to protect them from the burning sunshine.

Calton

Calton and his father had hardly spoken since Calton's mother had passed to the other side. Instead of remembering together, their attention was conveniently solicited by a constant flow of friends, neighbours and the congregation of The Holy Family Church who hesitated on the porch of the single story white clapboard house before they tapped on the screen door, offering condolences to the poor, motherless boy who answered it. From the day after Elizabeth died, it was always the boy who greeted them. The widower had taken to hiding in his bedroom.

"Calton. I'm so sorry for your loss. Elizabeth will be truly missed. It's all so terribly sad."

Dorothy scratched the itch on her left calf with the toe of her right foot, being careful not to ladder her stockings. If it wasn't for the casserole pot in her hands, she'd have enveloped the boy's skinny frame in her stouter arms. She held up the dish.

"I made you a beef stew. All you need do is heat it up, love."

Calton followed Dorothy as she strode down the hallway that ran along the whole right hand side of the house, past the three closed bedroom doors. She peeked in the living room and the study, listened for movement as she tried to work out where the widower was. Apparently he hadn't been seen since Father O'Reilly had visited on the previous Wednesday. In the kitchen she hesitated in front of the three casserole pots that sat on the stove, then put hers on the table and started lifting lids. She recoiled as the second one unleashed a smell putrid enough to make her gag.

"Do you have a refrigerator?"

Calton pointed to where the larder door was half open. They'd bought a brand new Cosley six months earlier. After years of hankering, his mother had been so thrilled with it she kept showing Cal how the light went on inside it when she opened it and made him listen to the clunk of the door as it shut. She put his hand on the bottle of milk she'd pulled off the second shelf.

"Feel how cold that is. It's incredible. Can you believe it? In our kitchen? It's like a miracle."

Calton swallowed hard. Her dying after they'd bought the refrigerator wasn't right, a person waiting ten years for something only for death to steal them away before they'd had the chance to take it for granted. How could that be fair? What sort of God would be so mean as to do that to a person?

"How's your father?" Dorothy asked as she put her pot in the refrigerator and emptied the contents of the others into the bin.

"Alright."

"You can tell him I'm here."

Calton lolloped down the hallway and knocked on his parents' bedroom door.

"Mrs Franklin's here, from church." When there was

no answer he slipped inside the room, shutting the door behind him. He knew their guest would be listening in order to repeat to the Women's Institute all she managed to hear. "Dad."

Mr Jonas was lying with his back to his son, on top of the blanket his dead wife had crocheted eleven years ago. His body covered the bright orange, red, blue, yellow and green patches. Elizabeth had preferred primary colours. She told Calton they released an energy that pastel shades sapped away. Calton's dad was still wearing the maroon jumper he'd put on to ward off the chill minutes before his wife had died. She'd touched its sleeve, dripped the last of the love from her fingertips onto the wool as the pain in her chest had won, suffocating her need for oxygen.

"Dad," Calton said louder. "I don't think she's going to leave without seeing you. You know what she's like." He bit his lower lip and scowled at his father. He knew he shouldn't be cross because after all he'd only been a widower for nine days but for Christ's sake couldn't he get up for once and not leave it to his son to sort out everything? "Dad," Calton barked, walking around the edge of the bed to face him.

Tucked up in Mr Jonas's arms like a new born babe was the silver framed photograph of Elizabeth and him that had been taken on their wedding day. They were laughing, holding hands, an infectious joy bursting through the glass screen. On the pillow, level with his closed eyes, was a folded note with the word CALTON written in capital letters as if the author had wanted to make sure his son was the only one to read it. From his partly open mouth came nothing: no breath, no whimper, no cry. Cal snatched the note and shoved it into his trouser pocket.

"Mrs Franklin." He hurried behind the bed, stood next to the door, his back against the brown painted wall. "Mrs Franklin! Mrs Franklin! Can you come here please?" Thick set calves ran towards his anxiousness. She opened the door. Her head appeared next to the boy's shoulder. "I think he's gone."

"Gone where?" she retorted. "He's right there."

"To be with mum. I think he's dead."

Dorothy crept towards the body as if worried she'd wake it. She peered at the corpse then placed her hand over the lips hoping to feel a slight breeze. Seconds later she made a sign of the cross.

"Rest in peace. In the name of the Father and the Son and the Holy Spirit. Amen."

She pulled the blanket from under Mr Jonas's legs, covered his face and torso with the brightness and her lips pinched together as she looked pityingly at the orphan who was staring at the green, linoleum floor.

"His heart must have broken. Imagine that. I guess it shows how much he loved your mother."

~

Dorothy sat opposite Father O'Reilly, filling him in as opposed to gossiping, she would never lower herself to that. Her words had a purpose compared to idle tittle-tattle.

"He's all alone. It's so dreadfully sad. More cake or would you rather a biscuit?"

"Cake please."

"It was a broken heart, that's what they're saying."

She sighed, wishing someone would love her enough to literally break once she'd passed away. After visiting the

Jonas house, she'd found her husband asleep on the sofa. She remembered how when they first met she always looked forward to seeing him whereas now she was ambivalent as to whether he returned home from work or not each evening. If she died, would he give up his life in such a fantastically romantic way? Or would he carry on, find happiness, perhaps a new love. And would she give up hers for him? She wasn't sure she would. The shame of it.

"I could come with you Father. It might be nice to have a woman there too. I could make some tea, bring a—"

"That's awfully kind of you Dorothy, really. But I think it's best I see him alone, man to man as it were."

"Right. Alright then but only if you're sure Father because—"

"This is such a delicious cake. Is that a hint of cinnamon I'm tasting? Sure you've a rare talent. Always the lightest sponge out of all of my visits."

~

Father O'Reilly sat at Calton's dining room table, hiding his shame at what Bishop Murphy had confirmed, that if there was even the slightest shadow of a doubt as to how Mr Jonas had died and unfortunately in this case there was a tsunami of it, then the father could not be buried in the churchyard next to where Calton's mother lay. Which seemed terribly cruel to Father O'Reilly. Because they were a decent family. Elizabeth had never missed a Sunday mass, not even when she'd given birth to the little one, not even near the end when her bones weren't strong enough to hold her up, the muscles non-existent from the ravaging illness that had destroyed her, wasting her physicality away. And for the last three weeks of her life she'd

13

asked the Father to visit her after mass so she was up-to-date with all her forgiveness and forgiving when she headed upstairs to meet her maker. She was a good woman. And had been happy with life, was horrendously upset to be going so early. Which must have meant her husband was also a good man. She clearly loved him and he adored her from the way he watched her as he hovered in the doorway when she was well enough for a guest, making tea, gently, very gently helping her to sit up, wincing as she grimaced at the pain of his hands on her shoulders while their gangly son fluffed air into the pillows.

He heard Calton stirring the tea. That poor wee boy. Eighteen was too young to have no-one to guide you. Father O'Reilly and the church would help him though of course there was the chance Calton would be furious when he was told they wouldn't accept the body. But it was out of Father O'Reilly's hands. The Bishop had insisted they couldn't let the spirit of the father rest in the sacrosanct graveyard.

Jesus wept.

Where the hell was the love of the church when such a young member of the congregation needed it? In the name of the Father and the Son and the Holy Spirit, dear Lord forgive me for swearing, in the name of the Father and the Son and the Holy Spirit, Amen. But it wasn't right, it didn't seem fair. Father O'Reilly knew the church had their reasons but it could turn a teenager to the dark side, they had to understand that.

"Do you take sugar Father?"

"No thanks Cal. As it is will be grand."

"Oh. Sorry. I put two in it. That's how mum and dad liked theirs."

"And that's grand too. What a treat! I only say no as otherwise Mrs Jenkins, you've met my housekeeper, she has a go at me, tells me I've enough weight on my belly without the tea adding to it." He patted his stomach but Calton didn't laugh. "That's delicious. You've made it just right. Thank you. Are you not having one yourself now?"

"No."

Calton sat opposite Father O'Reilly, hands under the table, fingertips rat-a-tat-tatting on his thighs, one of which was moving up and down super-fast as he counted in his head, one, two, three, four, five, six, seven, eight, one, two, three, four, five, six, seven, eight, one, two, three, four, five, six, seven, eight.

"So then. How are you?"

Calton stopped the twitching.

"Fine thank you Father."

Then started again. One, two, three, four, five, six, seven, eight.

"Good on you, though it can't be an easy time." Calton frowned. Father O'Reilly sipped more tea then put the cup down and pushed it towards the middle of the table, out of temptations way. "The reason I'm here Cal, the funeral, it—"

"I can wear the same suit again can't I? That's not disrespectful? I was worried you'd think it was."

"God no, not disrespectful at all. Your mother would be thrilled to see you getting wear out of it. I mean not like that but, you know. She'd be ever so proud of you. And your father would. Like the whole congregation is. And they, I, all of us, we're here if you need us." He didn't usually nearly cry, being so used to death and sadness, but this one had got to him.

"For what?"

"Anything. A hot meal, a bit of company, an ear to listen."

"I'm doing alright thanks."

"You are. We know you are. And—"

"Though I do miss them. The house is too quiet. It was meant for a family not me on my own. It's too big for that."

Father O'Reilly took a deep breath in. "Do you mind if I smoke?"

"No."

"Would you like one?"

Cal accepted the cigarette and took the Father's cup off its saucer, pointing to it when the match had been blown out.

"We can use that as the ashtray."

"Do you have any whiskey?"

Cal opened the mahogany sideboard, put a half empty bottle on the table and after that, two cut crystal glasses. Father O'Reilly poured, gulped, then poured more into his one. He sucked hard on his cigarette.

"I was thinking we could have it next Thursday if that suits you. Is it only local people or do some of their friends need to travel?"

"We never left here. Everyone's from town."

The Father nodded. "Right. Did your mammy have an address book? Maybe a list of people she sent Christmas cards to each year? They might need time to plan their journeys."

"No," Cal lied, too tired to face calling strangers. "She always said here was her home and what more did she need what with the church and dad and me coming along, the icing on the cake all those years later."

"Right. There we go then. So that's easy enough." Father O'Reilly stubbed his cigarette out in the saucer, brain whirring as it thought of what to tell the Bishop. Did he even need to tell him anything? Would he find out? It was a tricky one, these things had a way of spreading. "Next Thursday it is. Shall we say a start time of eleven?"

Susan

A coiled spring bent beneath Susan's fury. She punched
the mattress so hard for so long that a permanent dip
curved where her feet rested at night time. The plan was
for more money if they died. She'd planned it so carefully
and now it had been spoilt and her room had been poisoned by her sister. She would have to swap, move to
another one. She couldn't bear the thought of lying where
Alice's legs had touched, breathing the air her sister had
breathed back into. It was Susan's air, not meant for sharing. Since she'd moved in, no-one else had been in the
room and now Alice had come and spoilt it. Stupid little
sister.

~

The administration block was at the back of the hospital,
next to the canteen. Susan was the first in line when the
door was opened by a man with light brown hair and a
too long fringe that he kept flicking off his eyelashes. The
man stepped back, not expecting a visitor so early, so close
to him. Her breath was warm.

"Are you in charge of the nurses accommodation?"

"Amongst other things." The lady stared hard at him. "I look after the administration offices as well and when the hospital has visitors who need to stay over I—"

"How important you are," Susan declared as she stepped into the room. It was smaller than it looked from the outside with one grey metal desk facing the door, a grey metal filing cabinet behind that, a set of brass keys hanging out of the top lock. The floor squeaked under her nurse's shoes, toes protected, heel low. She sat in the wooden chair that faced the desk. "I wonder if you'd be so kind as to help me."

The administrator watched her shapely legs, nice ankles, beautiful dark hair, wondering what it felt like to stroke it. Was it long when it was free from the confines of the nurse's cap? How far would it cascade down her shoulders?

"I need to change rooms. I'm in the Charterhouse block, number thirty eight, second floor, right at the stairs then second door on the left. I need to move out of that room as soon as possible please, this evening preferably."

The administrator burst out laughing and when she didn't join in, sat behind his desk, facing her.

"You're serious?"

"Of course. Why wouldn't I be?"

"Do you have someone to swap with?"

"What do you mean?"

"Have you got a friend you want to swap with, or a friend's neighbour, that's what most girls want."

"No."

"Oh."

"You can sort it out for me."

"Excuse me?"

"Isn't that your job? You've made out like you're important. If you're as skilled as you think you are then surely
you can arrange this little thing?"

He coughed at her directness, or was it rudeness? She
was a bit like his mother, bossing him around though his
mother used a sweeter tone, more cajoling than com-
manding.

"My shift's about to start," said Susan. "What time will
you have my answer at?"

"What time do you finish?"

"Four o'clock."

"I'll try and let you know by then."

"Good. I'll be here at approximately seven minutes past
four, by the time I walk from the ward."

His smirking irked. She kicked her chair as she stood
up.

"I can't promise anything," he called out after her.

~

Susan had picked nursing as a career because there
weren't many jobs a girl could do that meant a steady
income plus guaranteed work in whatever town she
decided to move to in the state, the country, perhaps the
world. She'd done her research, read that the wage
increased with an annual increment, plus an inflationary
raise. If she was careful with the money, spent none apart
from on the most basic of essentials, she could save up,
cover her back for emergencies, buy a place once an
inheritance from her parents came through except now
the bastards had left her virtually high and dry. She
couldn't bear her quarters much longer with the squeal-
ing voices, dirt rimmed baths, soiled kitchen worktops,

no sense of hygiene within the place even after all the lectures they'd had about washing your hands and germs, stopping contagion from spreading. How could a person leave a dirty saucepan in the sink for someone else to clean before using it? It made no sense. Did they not think? Were they not conscious of their selfishness in assuming another person would clear up after them, another nurse who was just as busy as them thank you very much, they were all working shifts don't you know, don't you know, they were all exhausted. She couldn't stay there. There'd even been faeces in the toilet the other day. She couldn't comprehend how a decent person could do that. They weren't decent. They were loud, annoying, loud, too giggly for her liking, and loud, so loud. It wouldn't do. It was driving her crazy.

~

The administrator wasn't in his office. Susan kicked the door. Just after four was what they'd agreed and it was seven minutes past four now so she was dead on time. She kicked it again, twice for joy. It shook on its rusted hinges.

"Sorry. Sorry, I'm here. I'm coming." He was eating potato chips, dropping clusters on the ground, nearly as many as those that were making it into his mouth. "You're an impatient one."

"I beg your pardon?"

His grin froze in front of her scowl.

"Here we go then. Take a seat." He dropped the nearly empty packet into the grey metal bin at the side of his desk. Some of the crumbs fell onto the floor. Rats, thought Susan. There'll be rats all over the place, god-damn it.

More slovenly hygiene. Who raised these people? "I checked all the lodgings and thought we might be in luck as Merchant Hall was meant to be having a girl about to leave as she was all homesick the other week but turns out she's staying as the town's better than being back on the farm. She's got three brothers and no social life there so—"

"You're blathering. What's your point? Can I move or not? Do you have another room for me?"

"No."

"Why not?"

"I just told you."

"No you didn't. You just talked about some farm girl. They can't all be full."

"I'm afraid they are."

"Afraid of what?"

"Excuse me?"

"You're of no use, useless, less use than I need, not even trying, that's what I reckon. I've a good mind to report you." She stormed out and shut the door behind her then opened it and shrieked. "You don't even know what's driven me to this, what made me need to move, desperate for a different space. You didn't even ask. Why didn't you ask? Maybe I would have told you." She slammed it shut so hard it bounced back open again.

Jeffrey's hands shook as he unlocked the filing cabinet and picked out a bottle of whiskey that was hidden behind M for medicinal. He took three slugs in quick succession. He'd never been shouted at before, not by a girl. Women weren't meant to shout at men. That wasn't right. That wasn't allowed, surely. He'd never heard his mother shout at his father. Barbed comments, yes, little sneers perhaps but she'd never screamed at him like that nurse just did. He gulped down another seven mouthfuls then screwed the lid back on before finishing the day's paperwork.

~

Susan tossed from side to side, furious with that man. How dare he not have a room. How dare he smirk. How on earth could he eat and speak at the same time. So rude. Was no-one taught manners anymore? People were so dirty and disgusting. And it wasn't fair that she needed him in order to have somewhere to sleep at night, that he had such control over her life like his bosses over her wages. It riled. Bastards the lot of them.

~

Every nurse knew to leave her alone. The fury emanated from every pore, warning the world not to go near her, don't dare say a word. Not even the Matron intervened when Susan pulled Martha Jenkin's arms too roughly as she helped her sit up to use the bedpan. Martha cowered, her translucent skin marked red from the strong fingers gripping it hard enough to stain while being careful not to actually snap the eighty three year old bones.

"Finished?"

"Yes. Thank you. Sorry Nurse."

"You should have gone when everyone else did, making my life hard, like it's not difficult enough already with all of you lot to look after."

"Sorry."

Martha decided she didn't like that nurse with the dark, dark eyes. She'd tell her son about the mean one when he came to visit which he was sure to do one day soon, like he'd promised.

~

Susan sat on her bed, listening to Rachel's music through the walls, the same record being played over and over, the floor shaking as Rachel bounced along to the piano part.

She would have to find a man. That was the only solution she could think of. There was no other way she'd escape from shared living though it would still be shared but at least only with one person rather than sixty nine others. She'd smile and be nice to a man, one with a steady wage, preferably no family so they didn't have to visit and put up with his parents, brothers, sisters. The thought of that was excruciating and enough to put Susan off but she decided she could, she must, be prepared to deal with it. If he did have a family, she'd make herself appear submissive enough for them to fall for her. And as it was her plan it meant she was the one in control even though he'd think he was the one in charge. She'd put up with a husband like her mother had her father except she wouldn't have children. The reason for the relationship was purely to get an apartment, not to love or be loved, there was no need for any of that nonsense.

Susan

The administrator watched the nurse who'd wanted the new room and wished he was in his car rather than travelling on the bus as if he was too poor to own one. They should make more parking spaces available to all the staff at the hospital. And he was staff, not a doctor or a surgeon but a person of worth who kept the wheels turning behind their gaudy shows. They should be grateful he existed for without him there'd be no nurses living free from their parents, looking for dates to take them to the dances, to feel them up down the alleyways.

There was no denying the curve of the calf and the nip of the waist he was sure her hair was long enough to fall onto. There was a seat next to him but she chose to stand, letting a middle aged lady in a blue dress take what should have been her place. She obviously hadn't seen him, hadn't noticed his new red tie yet.

~

Susan made herself stare out of the window even though she wanted to watch him, to check if his pallor was healthy, his hair shiny, none of his teeth rotten or missing. Her stop came too quickly. She turned to smile with a surprised *oh you* to acknowledge his presence but he was looking at his knees so she hurried out of the doors, embarrassed by her obviousness and lack of experience.

As she walked through the hospital grounds a boy's voice called, "Miss, Miss!" The lady with the walking stick who'd got off the bus infuriatingly slowly but with some help from Susan's right arm said, "I think he means you love," with a twinkle in her eye. Susan turned and was rewarded with awkward mumblings.

"It's me, from the office. We met the other day when you came about your room. I was wondering, perhaps you'd maybe, I don't know, we could—"

"What?"

"Would you like to go for dinner one night?"

Look at her skill, making him want to date her.

"What's your name?"

"Jeffreys."

"Your first name."

"Jeffrey."

"Surname?"

"Jeffreys."

"Jeffrey Jeffreys?" she laughed. "Why did they call you that? That's ridiculous."

"I know. I don't know. I often wonder what they'd have called a second child."

"You've no brothers or sisters?"

"No. You?"

She hesitated. "No." He had all his teeth, stained yellow so he was probably a smoker. She checked his fingers, brown and yellow splodges between the index and middle finger of his right hand but that was fine. It meant he'd die younger. "I'll come to dinner."

"Really? Excellent." His body relaxed as he grinned.

"As long as you find me a room, prove that you're worth something."

He laughed like she was joking.

"Pah." She folded her arms and looked at his shoes. The brown leather was polished, a strong crease in the trouser legs that rested on them. He was well kept.

"You're serious?"

"Why wouldn't I be?"

She bent one knee in slightly, the movement taking his attention to her ankles. She made herself smile. She had good teeth, better than his, straight, more white than beige.

"I'll try my best. When are you free?"

"Tomorrow night."

"What's your address?"

He picked out a piece of paper from his briefcase and balanced on one leg, placing the case on his raised knee, the paper on top of that. So he was stupid, not remembering the number of the room and the building she'd told him she lived in only a few days ago. Stupid would do, stupid would make life easier. He didn't wobble as he wrote. She wondered if she could balance as well as him or had he practiced. Was that a skill a hospital administrator needed? Maybe. Maybe he had to balance when he went round the staff quarters checking for leaks and unwanted behaviour. He screwed the lid back on his fountain pen and in one fluid movement lowered his leg, flicked the paper through the air so the ink dried then shut her details safely in his brown leather case.

He'd do.

They could work for each other.

Two odd souls who'd pretended they'd touched and

cared. She'd lied when asked by the other nurses how she preferred to hold a boy's hand. She said, "cupped of course" when they insisted on an answer, blocking the door so she couldn't leave the kitchen until she'd told them. That was how she'd once held her father's hand as a child. But that was wrong. They all said they preferred intertwined fingers, no spaces, no air between the skin. Susan didn't care about not having held a hand but she did care about her answer being wrong. Jeffrey had lied when asked by the other boys at the Christmas party what titties he liked best. "Oh you know," he'd said nonchalantly, never having touched or kissed a pair. If he'd been honest and said it was the eyes he thought were more important, wouldn't they have thought him even odder than they already did. He hoped she couldn't read his mind but when he scanned her face she was watching his hands. Her eyes were nearly black. She looked at his mouth rather than his eyes before turning round to walk to the main entrance.

A bus belched noisily behind him as it braked, making him jump. He checked his watch. It had only taken four minutes. He would still be on time for work. It was a good thing.

~

That evening Susan flicked through the three dresses she owned, black, navy and brown, for the first time wishing she had more to choose from. Her bubble of satisfaction deflated as she pictured herself looking drab on her first ever date. She went to the kitchen for some water and decided against eating any dinner. She wanted to be slim for him.

Rachel Pewter was sitting at the table eating a bowl of cereal. Susan re-filled her glass with water. She imagined her and Jeffrey sitting in a cinema, walking in the park, going for dinner in a restaurant, a glass of wine on the table. They'd fit right in. They could look normal.

"Are you alright?"

Susan didn't like the way Rachel spoke with her mouth full but decided to be gracious.

"Yes."

Rachel swallowed and smiled.

"You look different."

"Excuse me?"

"Something's different. I have a sixth sense about these things." Some cereal fell off her lips, onto the table. She used her thumb to pick it up and put it back in the bowl. "Oh my god, you're blushing. What's his name? Was he at the dance? No, you weren't there. How then? Where did you meet him? Are you going out later?"

Susan bristled at the intrusion. "It's none of—"

"Are you? You must be. Dancing, eating, or cinema?"

"To a restaurant."

"Fabulous."

Rachel banged her spoon on the edge of the table as if applauding. Susan studied Rachel's expression but didn't think she was mocking her.

"I'm not sure what to wear," she admitted.

"Oh, you'll think of something." Rachel concentrated on pouring more Rice Krispies into her bowl and turned the page of her magazine.

~

There was a knock on Susan's door. She pulled the bolt back and was greeted by a mountain of scarves, bags and hats. Rachel poked her head out from behind them.

"You're half the size of me so none of my dresses will fit but it's amazing what can be done with accessories."

In she walked without being asked, throwing her goodies on the bed. The skin prickled on Susan's neck but she decided to contain her natural animosity. She wished Rachel wasn't in her room but if she caught this boy she'd have to get used to sharing square footage. On went an air of false enthusiasm. After looking at Susan's three dresses, Rachel picked the brown one with tiny dark purple flowers dotted all over it, so small they looked almost buried beneath the soil.

"This we can work with."

Susan held the frock unsurely, tormented at having to undress in front of someone. Sensing her discomfort, Rachel turned to face the wall and by trying to change too quickly, Susan stumbled.

"Shit."

Rachel laughed and turned around.

"My God, look at your figure."

So Susan's restraint at mealtimes was worthwhile. She stood as still as a shop mannequin while Rachel dressed her in hats, scarves, bags and belts. Susan wasn't allowed to look in the mirror until the words "et voila!" were shouted dramatically, loud enough for the whole floor to hear. Rachel changed the angles of the three mirrored dressing table so Susan could see herself from head to toe and front to side.

She looked suave like the ladies in magazines. There was a clip in her hair with a large silver flower on it, matching the silver scarf tied *just so* around her neck and the sparkling clutch bag under her arm.

"Tres glamorous! You look fabby." Rachel gathered up

her bits. "What shoes are you wearing? Have you got any heels?"

"No."

"What size are you?"

"A three."

"Seriously? Jesus. Okay, leave it with me." She hooked the door open with her hip and strode happily down the hall.

Susan shut and locked her door then stared at the stranger in the mirror, taking in every detail so she could replicate it the next night. She carefully undressed, hanging the outfit in the wardrobe and lay awake for two hours trying to predict the following evening.

~

The day dragged. Every time Susan checked the clock it was only a few minutes later than at the previous glance. She felt like smashing its face to stop the teasing tick tocks, snapping the hands that were strangling her. She clenched Peter Stephens' stainless steel bedpan as she hurried to empty it then banged it down so hard that some of his urine spilt on her arm as well as her apron. Kicking the cabinet five times she muttered, "damn fucker," over and over. Susan hadn't been so angry in days. She leant against the door so no-one could come in; if they did she'd cause a row. She focused on controlling the fury. Slowly. Slowly it fell to the floor and she was able to scrub her arms and re-enter the world. She checked the clock on the ward, seventeen minutes had passed but the Sister hadn't noticed her missing.

When she got back to her room, a pair of silver shoes were by the door. A pink paper note said, 'these are a four, stuff with cotton wool. Can't wait to hear all about it!!! Rachel. x'. Susan had never worn a heel so high. There was an inch of spare space from her longest toes to the edge of the leather. She ran to the toilet and pulled off lots of pieces of paper from the roll, shoving more and more into the shoes until they felt snug on her feet. She wanted them tight rather than loose, in case she slipped and made a fool of herself. When she saw them in the mirror she admired how they emphasised her slender ankles and after dressing she turned slowly to check her reflection at all three angles.

"Good."

It was twenty to eight. So she didn't crease the dress or ladder her palest tights, she stayed standing and waited for the buzzer to ring.

Calton

Cal slipped on the jacket of the black suit his father had bought him to wear to his mother's funeral. He caught some hairs in his watch strap so unclasped it before carefully clicking it shut again. It had been his eighteenth birthday present: silver, masculine, expensive, engraved C. J. He'd felt his mother's ribs through the skin on her back when he'd hugged her gently to say thank you for such a beautiful gift, you shouldn't have.

After the eleven o'clock service the mourners walked to the hotel that Cal's best friend's dad owned, where he'd offered a room for the reception, food and booze all for free. It'd be wrong to charge an orphan.

~

Cal accepted the cigarette proffered by the slurring Father.

"Sometimes you can feel like it's the end of the world. But it's not. I know it's hard Cal but you have to put one foot in front of the other and march on. One day you'll arrive at a place you hadn't planned on, that you hadn't expected to see and your adventure will be all the better for a wander because without expectation there's no disappointment, merely an acceptance of how you got there."

"Health is wealth," added Dorothy. "Without health what use is anything? Nothing. And I'll tell you that for free."

Cal excused himself and went to look for Johnny.

As far as he could see, you were born and you died and there was a chunk in between of course but once you were gone you were gone and years later some people might remember you but to what end as you were dead, your soul was over. What they remembered meant nothing.

"How are you doing young Calton? You look a bit peaky." Tom Irving plucked a white cotton handkerchief from his pocket to wipe some sweat from his brow. "Christ it's a hot one. Do you want to head off with Johnny for a bit, hit the water, clear your head? I can look after this lot."

"Yeah?" His parents might disapprove of him surfing on such a solemn day. "Maybe. Excuse me a minute Sir."

As he hurried down the corridor to the bathroom, the leather soles of his new shoes slipped on the polished, dark wooden floor. He carried on, trying to maintain some dignity before he hid in one of the two cubicles in the men's room, curled up on top of the seat. He pushed his fist into his mouth so as to not scream. The main door banged against a wall.

"He's lucky mind. I heard the insurance money paid off the mortgage leaving plenty to spare. I'd rather have had that at eighteen than be left with bloody oldies like mine to look after." Urine was pissed against the tiles. A man burped. "Jesus Ryan. Have you been eating the fish? That fucking stinks."

A third man entered but his footsteps sounded as if they'd gone to the sinks rather than the urinals.

"Alright?" Tom asked the two guests.

"Right. Nice do," Jason slurred.

"God bless and all that," said Ryan. He burped again, for longer than before.

Cal's eyes flickered from left to right as he wished they'd leave. He held his breath and gripped the sides of the cubicle walls so as to not risk falling, giving away that he was in there.

"How much do you reckon it's worth Tom?" asked Ryan.

"What?"

"The house," said Jason.

"Which house?" Tom said, knowing full well what they meant.

"The boy's. I reckon it'd be—"

"Why would you care? You want to buy it?"

"I wish."

"Hey. Wash your hands. There's food being passed around out there. I don't want you being the reason my pub gets blamed for—"

"We heard he's getting money as well as the house." A tap started running. "From the insurance and stuff. We were wondering, do you think he'd be interested in investing? It's a solid proposition. We're looking at opening a golf club up where the quarry used to be."

"Leave the lad alone."

"But—"

"For Christ's sake. He just lost both his parents. Leave him be. Go on. Get out of here. Scoot."

The floor of the cubicle was darkened by shadows. There was a grunt before two of them left the room. Stubby hands appeared on the floor, under the door, then a chin and an eye that couldn't see him.

"Calton? Is that you in there?" said Tom.

Cal pulled his thighs closer into his chest. The enormity of being all alone was terrifying. No-one in the world but him would remember what his mum's voice sounded like. No-one except Cal knew the smell of her perfume or his dad's aftershave that he kept for Sundays and the occasional Saturday night out, and his dad's whistle when he walked up the path on his way home from work, his mum's singing when one of her favourite songs came on the radio. She'd had a good voice but now she and dad were dead no-one else on the planet would ever know that, which meant when Cal died, and one day he too would definitely die, his mum and dad would be wiped from the earth forever. Someone would throw their boxes of photos out and phish, gone, as if they'd never existed. How was it possible to be on the earth one minute and gone forever the next? It didn't make sense. There had to be more to it otherwise what was it all about and what was the point of it.

"Don't mind them Cal. They've had too much free beer. It makes blokes talk a load of nonsense. Funerals and weddings, people always end up talking shit, not thinking. Someone always gets too drunk and puts their foot in it."

Cal wiped the tears from his face and his watch face, not wanting it damaged from getting wet. When the hands under the door pulled back, Cal let his feet drop onto the floor and bowed his head. What would he do when he went home? Who would he talk to? What was the point of getting up tomorrow? The door banged shut. A few minutes later there was a squeak as it was pushed open.

"Cal. Cal, it's Johnny mate. Are you alright?"

Cal sniffed. "Yeah."

"Do you want to go for a surf? Dad said he'll cover for us."

Cal kept sniffing.

"He's even given us some beers. I reckon we should get going before Mum finds out. You know what she's like."

Cal half laughed and blew his nose. He undid the latch on the door so it swung open.

"What do you say? Shall we do one?"

He nodded.

~

They stopped by Cal's house where he changed into blue shorts and a white T-shirt and shunted his surf board on the back seat of Johnny's car. Cal put his sunglasses on. Johnny overtook every car they got stuck behind, desperate to get to the beach, wanting the sea breeze to lighten his friend's heaviness.

"The Wreck or the Pass?"

"The Pass."

Cal hoped there'd be a nasty sweep, figuring he had nothing to lose if it dragged him to the bottom of the ocean and kept him there.

Johnny turned right towards the lighthouse. The swell was nowhere near big enough for the danger Cal craved. He lay on his board, watching the sun play on the water. He was tempted to dive down to the sea bed, tie himself to a rock, be at peace like his parents now were. He'd read the note. His dad was happy now; alright for him, the selfish bastard. Dolphins bobbed around them, hungry for an evening feed.

"This is shit. Fancy a beer?" asked Johnny.

As Cal got the fire going, Johnny rolled a joint. Cal craned his neck to check behind his friend, down the beach.

"You'll like this. It's mellower than the last lot," said Johnny. He offered Cal the first toke. "After the day you've had, Jesus mate, the month you've had, it'll do you good. It's all so fucked up man."

Cal inhaled and leant his back against a rock. Johnny poked at the fire with a stick.

"Mum says you're to stay at ours tonight. I said it's up to you but she's got a bee in her bonnet about it, says she doesn't want you being home alone and stuff."

Cal thought of his dark, empty house. What if his dad's ghost was in the bedroom, looking for his mum's soul which was four miles away at the hospital if it stays in the spot where you died which it must do. Was that right? Was that what the priest had said? Two dolphins played hide and seek. His mum would have pointed them out though he could easily see them. She loved the ocean, walked along it every evening even if there was rain lashing out. They should have burned her and scattered her ashes into the air and water so she could fly and float off, exploring the planet in a way she never got the chance to when she was alive. Being buried would drive her crazy; all that dirt she'd be wanting to clean up all the time, unable to stand the soil and bugs dribbling through the cracks in the coffin, into her new home. And her husband being constantly beside her. That would irk. When he'd had weekends off work he'd follow her round the house, getting in her way when she was trying to get on with her tidying. It worked better when he was at the office all day and home for the evening. That's how a marriage was meant to be.

"My Dad left a note."

"Yeah? Shit man, I—"

"Not that sort of note. Just saying stuff, nice stuff, about how much he loved mum and all that."

"Right. That is nice," Johnny said, unsure. He gestured for Cal to pass it here.

Cal handed over the spliff and took a swig of beer. It was nice, the note, sort of. It also felt mean, the note, sort of, as it let the son know his parents would be happy together, without him. They were leaving their boy alone on earth while they danced under the stars and explored heaven, chatted to God and all the famous people they'd always wanted to meet who'd passed on before them. A written word was powerful, more so than a spoken one that can be forgotten or misremembered. A letter could be re-read and unless it was burnt or ripped to shreds, taken by the binmen by accident or on purpose, it was never lost. Re-reading it each evening, in the mornings, when he was sitting in a chair staring at the walls, that made Cal veer between feeling very empty, very angry, then very sad then very selfish for wanting them both back with him, and finally, furious. He'd mutter they were a pair of bastards, not mum, except for his mum because her going wasn't on purpose. She'd fought until the very end, so much so that Cal had said let go now mum, it's too painful watching you struggle and she did, just like that, one minute breathing desperately, the next minute she'd stopped and there was no going back from the death that had taken her.

"Hey. Scoot." Johnny waved away the girl who was staring at them. She had curly dark hair and brown eyes, skin golden from days and days on the beach, in the sun.

She raised her fingers to her mouth, pretending to smoke like the boys were, bending her hip like the ladies in magazines. Johnny grabbed a handful of sand and threw it at her feet. "Go on. Get out of here. I mean it."

She turned and ran, kept running, far down the beach then left across it, over the dunes and up the hill.

~

Johnny waited in the living room while Cal packed a bag and took all the money from the jar in the back of the refrigerator. His mum had reckoned no burglars would ever look in there. He offered Johnny five dollars.

"What's that for?"

"Petrol."

"Nah. You're alright."

"And weed. Can you get us some more?"

"Ah. Of course. Now that I *can* take your money for."

Susan

Jeffrey drank a large glass of white wine before he picked up his car keys, finally ready to leave the house.

"See you later!"

"Have a good night," his father called back.

"Night darling. Love you," his mother added. "Drive safely."

He drove with both front windows down. The warm breeze blew his fringe over his eyes. He brushed it away then picked up the silver flask by the handbrake. When it was securely clamped between his thighs, he unscrewed the lid and after a few messy gulps he burped and whooped out loud. A group of teenagers whooped back, mocking his joy. Two wrong turns followed by a right one led to her road.

"Concentrate Jeffrey," he muttered to himself as he pull-ed up and parked. The house had twenty three windows on the face of its dark grey stone. A set of navy double doors were open, giving passers-by a peak at the gloomy interior. Some girls were sitting outside on the steps, smoking. Sober, he'd have recoiled at the thought of approaching them but confident with whiskey he strode straight up.

"Good evening ladies."

Two giggled, three stared and one replied, "Alright."

"I've come for…" He tried to think of her name. But he hadn't written it down.

"Me," said Susan.

Jeffrey's eyes widened and his shoulders relaxed as he realised he was relieved to find his date still attractive. Sparkly silver shoes led to stunning legs, a waist nipped in with a silver belt and loose hair that he wanted to touch, right away. He was right when he'd imagined how long it was.

"Wait!" A taller girl ran up the path. "Hang on."

She grabbed Susan's hand, pulling her inside so her ankle turned on the heel. A minute later they both re-appeared. His date's lips were now a deep, dark, devilish shade of red.

Susan put her hand on his arm. He moved it so they held hands, fingers cupped round each other. Susan changed the grip so their fingers were intertwined, as if she knew what she was doing. The bystanders gawped. They couldn't remember seeing Susan in make-up before, or heels, nothing remotely glamorous. Jeffrey opened the passenger door of the car and when he turned she was right in front of him, so close that their heads almost knocked together. He squeezed by, shut her door and walked to the driver's side, trying to hide his nervous-ness.

"I don't know your name." His voice span from a high note to baritone.

"Susan."

"That's pretty."

"You think?"

She repeated his words in her head. It was the first time 'pretty' had been used in a sentence about her.

"Susan what?"

"Smith. Susan Smith," she fibbed.

"Ha. I should have guessed that one."

She pretended to laugh with him as if he was funny and clever.

Jeffrey drove to the street in town where five restaurants sat in a row. All the nearby parking spaces were taken but Susan didn't mind. She would walk by his side, in public. When he opened her door he stood far back as if afraid. Susan boldly moved her hand into his and gently stroked his thumb like she'd seen other couples do. The hairs on his arms stood up. He needed a drink so hurried her towards *Il Posto*.

Susan had never eaten Italian food and hoped the dishes would agree with her delicate digestion. The red and white checked tablecloths were too bright but the darker walls and dim lighting suited. The waiter pulled out a chair for the lady. He filled their glasses with red wine from a terracotta jug. Jeffrey drank his whole glass in one go, sighed, re-filled it. He put on a silly voice.

"Forgive my manners, you've got me all flustered ma'am."

Susan drank four gulps of the wine, trying to match his pace. It was tepid. She stifled a cough, not wanting him to know she was unused to alcohol and drank more to ease the tickle. He refilled her glass, thrilled to have found a lady with a thirst like he had.

"Cheers," he said.

They clinked their glasses together. Red wine spilt on her thumb. She giggled like other nurses did. He giggled.

They relaxed a little as she let him talk about his job, her quarters, the chance of them meeting, of her needing a room and them both being on a bus together. She also let him order her food, the wine introducing a wilder side. The restaurant was busy, the service slow and by the time the bowl of pasta arrived Susan wasn't hungry. Her head felt wavy. The room tipped from side to side when she glanced at the other tables. Jeffrey raised his glass and downed his drink whilst simultaneously ordering another jug by pointing his hand at the empty one. His confidence was infectious. Susan pierced a square of ravioli and popped it in her mouth. The texture wasn't pleasant, a smooth slimy outer skin with a thicker, tough filling. She could tell it was meat from the way she had to chew it. Susan was very good at telling food from its texture. Because she could not taste.

Not since one mean push from her mother meant the whack on her head when she fell damaged a part of her brain so it no longer worked with her tongue to distinguish the flavours of whatever she put in her mouth. She wouldn't dwell on that now though. Instead she ate square after square until her plate was empty. And then, like him, she wiped the bread across the china to gather the sauce, accompanied by more wine. She felt uncomfortably full but he ordered a chocolate mousse to share. She'd pretend to eat, squash down the queasiness.

"Do you know where the bathroom is?"

Jeffrey frowned as if confused by her question. The waiter subtly pointed to his right. When Susan stood up, she had to put her hand on the table to steady herself. Either she or the room was swaying. Jeffrey laughed. Susan followed the wall the waiter had directed her past, concentrating hard on reaching the brown door with the picture of a girl in a blue and white swimsuit holding a red bucket and spade stuck onto it. She locked herself in a cubicle, leant against the partition, closed her eyes then immediately opened them as the spinning got worse.

"Damn it."

She was tempted to heave. But what if he wanted to kiss her, wanted to twirl his tongue around hers like the nurses said they'd done with their boyfriends, as they sat around the table in the kitchen, heads sore on Sunday mornings. What if he did that and she tasted of bile? He'd never want to see her again. She breathed deeply through her nose, willing a trapped burp to rise. She needed to pee. Not used to heels, Susan squatted to her normal pissing level then her knees buckled and she collapsed heavily onto the seat.

"Christ."

She banged her right fist on the cubicle wall then steadied herself by flattening both hands on either side. Liquid sprayed onto the ceramic bowl, the quiet told her she'd finished. She wiped and pulled up her underwear and tights. She flushed, unlocked, locked, unlocked the door and stumbled forwards, propelled by her heels to the sink and mirror. The lights around it were too bright; she preferred the darker eating area. The glare was unforgiving of a spot just below her lip and a second one above her left eyebrow. She tilted her head to the left, to the right, and decided to sit so only her right side faced Jeffrey as then he wouldn't see her imperfections. The ruby red lipstick had disappeared. She should have accepted Rachel's offer of borrowing it for the evening. She'd buy her own one. Susan laughed at her reflection, at how simple life had become, for every problem a solution. The room span wildly. She held onto the sink.

"Skirt's caught." A second reflection with blond, curly hair and brown eyes, an unusual combination, smiled at her. "Your skirt's caught up at the back."

Craning her neck, Susan saw her dress was hooked into her tights. She hastily pulled it out and checked the rest of her outfit. She ran her fingers under the cold tap and went back to their table. Jeffrey had re-filled her glass or hadn't she drunk it? She couldn't remember. She'd pretend to sip from now on.

"Coffee?" he asked.

Other nurses drank numerous cups before their shifts to sober up after a wild one. It might work for her. She nodded.

"Black or white?"

"White." Her mother and father used to scoop three sugars into theirs so she'd add none. She double checked she'd picked up the right glass then took a sip of water.

"Pacing yourself?" Jeffrey asked. "I get ya darling."

He winked. She drank more so as to not give away the fact that she detested winking.

The coffee arrived in a white tin pot. Susan felt the heat on her lips, teeth and tongue, a slight burn on the back of her throat but no flavour. A drip of dark liquid ran down Jeffrey's chin. Her head suddenly hurt.

"I need to go home now."

Jeffrey flicked his hand in the air. A minute later the waiter appeared with the bill. He felt unstoppable and when he proffered an arm, Susan was glad to lean on it, surprised to find that his skin was as soft as the underside of her knees and the hairs were as fine. She wondered if the hairs on his face were prickly and giggled at her nerve.

"What's so funny?"

He looked unsure. She gripped his hand. He squeezed hers back.

There were no nurses hanging round the house. Curtains were shut and lights were out. They floundered in that moment before the first kiss, before it gets complicated, then he leant forward and put his lips upon hers. When she pulled back he apologised then she kissed him, holding the back of his head with her hand. It was easier than she'd thought it would be. The moon lit them like movie stars and Jeffrey felt like a lead in life, full of confidence now another person wanted him. Susan ran her tongue in circles around his. He was tasteless, tongue like a slug. Enough. She put her key in the lock.

"Night then." She hovered in the open doorway. He got it.

"Can I see you again?"

"Friday. I'm not working the next day."

"Me neither. Friday's good. I'll pick you up at 7.30."

~

The next morning Susan's head hurt terribly. She got out her personal medicine bag that was wrapped in a green cardigan, third drawer down. There were plenty of pills to choose from, all pilfered from work over the last two years. She kept them for emergencies, giving patients placebos when she knew they weren't really ill.

She tried to find Rachel, asking the other girls if they knew what shift she was working that day but they shrugged, said no, carried on smoking their cigarettes. One asked how her date went. Susan shrugged too. She left a note under Rachel's door. Later that afternoon the reply said, 'radiant red, no 23, fine to keep hold of shoes

until Sat. Can't wait to hear all about your date!! Fabby!!!
xx'

~

Susan reached the pharmacy just before it was due to close, the bell ringing triumphantly as she passed through its soon to be locked door. Scented bubbles filled the shelves that led to the make-up counter; row upon row of coloured pencils, eye shadows and lipsticks. One of the display casings was familiar, the same packaging as Rachel's make-up. Susan ran her finger along the numbers until she reached 23. There was one last stick in the slot. She took it to the counter.

"Number nineteen, nice shade. One thirty nine please."

"Excuse me?"

"That's one thirty nine please."

The girl with poker straight, blond hair turned the lipstick over to double check the price even though she knew she was right.

"It's number twenty three, not nineteen."

"No. See." The assistant held up the base for Susan to read. "Nineteen, berry brown."

"But it was in the slot for twenty three."

"Oh, I'm sorry. People take them out to look at them then put them back in the wrong place."

The assistant infuriated Susan by smiling as if this was acceptable.

"Do you have a twenty three?"

"I'm not sure."

"You should know."

"We—"

"I need number twenty three."

"I—"

"I came here specifically to buy it and you made it look as if you have it but now you're saying you aren't sure. I haven't got time to waste you know."

The girl stepped back so her head pushed into the shelf behind her. The pharmacist looked down on the scene. Susan removed her hands from the counter. She needed their help.

"Perhaps you could check? Maybe you have one in stock?"

The insincere smile fooled no-one.

"The only place they'd be is in the rack."

"Is it possible there's a 23 in another hole?"

"I guess."

"It's a simple enough question, yes or no?"

"Yes." The pharmacist's voice was lower, firmer.

"Right. *I'll* check then."

Starting at number one Susan worked her way methodically along each row. She couldn't believe the muddle they were in. The assistant should be fired for incompetence. Susan re-ordered the strays, her irritation growing the further along the line she got. Then at number forty one she pulled out one with 23 on its base. She looked away and back again to make sure her eyes weren't playing tricks. There was 23 printed in black ink, the words 'radiant red' in a tiny, smudged font beneath it.

The find made her reckless. She picked up the smallest bottle of bubbles that were on sale and chose a 'Lily Dreams' scent so her neck smelled sweetly if Jeffrey kissed it. The pharmacist took her money. The assistant locked the door behind her, turning the sign to 'closed'.

"Prickly," she said to her boss.

~

Sitting on the edge of her bed, Susan pulled the film off the cylindrical tube. Susan's first lipstick. The navy lid came off with a satisfying pop. She swivelled up the stick. Radiant red span through the air, two sides meeting at a perfect tip, never touched. She checked it from every angle, sniffed to see if there was a flavour she would miss tasting but not catching any perfume. She twisted it back down, checking it was fully submerged before replacing the lid.

The bubble bath bottle had a petal shaped lid. This time a strong, sweet smell made her nose itch and a sneeze escape before she could swallow it. The bottle juddered in her hand but she managed not to spill any. She screwed the lid back on and placed both it and the lipstick on what had been her bare dresser. They looked out of place, too colourful and girlish. She sprayed some scent on her wrist and sniffed. Two sneezes this time but it would have to do.

If she played the administrator carefully, she could move on in life. Two wages were better than one and there'd be a name change. She'd become Mrs Susan Jeffreys. There we go. That had to make it worth the wooing.

Susan

Susan ran a bath, pouring one fifth of her bubbles under the piping hot tap. She recalled conversations she'd eavesdropped on fooling around, fingering and fucking. The last word made her flinch. It sounded hard and mean but she needed a route out and if that was the way to get it then that's what she'd do. She pouted at the tiles, trying to be sexual but felt a fake. It would be easier after wine. She rubbed the bubbles vigorously over her skin. The blurb on the bottle said the nut oil would make it smooth. Her hand moved under her arms, a finger caught in some hair.

"Damn it."

She knocked on doors until the sixth one was answered. Susan raised her right arm and pointed to the dark mass underneath it. The girl looked appalled, disappearing for a few seconds before coming back with a razor.

"Keep it."

Susan ran back to the bathroom. She flicked the lid off the blades. It was similar to the ones they used at the hospital; she'd shaved plenty of patients but never herself. The hairs were so long she sliced an inch off, then another.

The blade ran roughly over her skin leaving red marks where follicles opened up. She cupped bubbly water in one hand and threw it into the socket. It stung but helped the razor glide. She decided to shave her legs from hip to ankle. The hairs were fine and dim compared to those under her arms. She didn't carve a single cut.

After the water had drained, hundreds of dark hairs littered the white enamel bathtub like a mass of baby spiders free of their eggs. She ran more water and splashed it over the bath until not one strand remained. Then she dressed slowly as if for a funeral rather than a date: clean black bra and pants, black dress, silver shoes and Rachel's silver scarf. She wiped the red paste over her lips until they stood out boldly against her pale skin then blotted and re-applied like Rachel had done. She waited, standing up so as not to crease her dress.

~

Jeffrey had his first drink straight after his shower, his second while making small talk with his mother and his third in the car. In general, he started to relax after the third.

He had to park further away this time. There were lots of boys leaving their cars and each returned with a girl. Some ran and laughed, some looked nervous and shy, one pair was angry like a row was brewing. Jeffrey swigged from his flask, betting on which relationships would work and which would fall apart. He put the flask back under the cloth, under his seat and went to ring the buzzer. The door was wedged open with a telephone directory. He hesitated, not wanting to go in. It was too female a world for him. He knocked and waited. About to knock again, he paused when a girl poked her head out of an open window on the first floor. Her disappointment was obvious but replaced by excitement when he heard footsteps on the gravel behind him. She waved and called out, "two ticks honey."

The boy behind him smiled, wiped his brow, ruffled his hair. Footsteps clattered down the stairs. The window girl ran straight into the boy's arms and they were immediately entwined, lips sealed with a long, luxurious kiss. Her eyes were closed but the boy's gazed upon her as if she were the most wondrous creature he'd ever seen. Their eyes locked when she opened hers and they walked hand in hand, arm in arm, her head on his shoulder.

That was what Jeffrey wanted.

He knocked harder this time and shouted down the hallway, "Susan. Hello? Susan!" Another window opened, another girl popped her head out, already dressed for bed in blue and white checked pyjamas, no disappointment on her face as she didn't have a date that night. A magazine and bag of aniseed twists would keep her company.

"I'm looking for Susan." She stared blankly at him. "Dark hair, slim, pretty in a way, a bit harsh looking."

"One second."

He heard shouts and calls through the open door. Voices tumbled through the corridors. He saw the silver shoes and stood straighter. His stomach grumbled nervously as his brain figured out how to greet her, wishing their instinct was to kiss like the couple before them.

"You look nice." He gestured to the path. "Shall we?" Susan held her hand out but he'd already turned around and started walking down the steps. "How about a drink before a film or would you rather something to eat? How was your week?"

"Bearable."

He persevered. Wine helped, a lot. They drank so much they missed the film and snacked on peanuts at the bar rather than heading to a restaurant. Susan reassured Jeffrey that a fancy meal was unimportant to her, a waste of money if anything. Though she drank less than Jeffrey her head span more. Inhibitions slipped away. She put her hand on his so he moved forward to kiss her, in public. His tongue was warm and wet again like the ravioli from the other night. He moved his free hand behind her head, imitating the couple on the drive. He pushed his groin against her. She pulled away.

"Not here."

Jeffrey downed his drink and gallantly pulled her to standing. The stack of empty glasses shook as they clumsily brushed past the ebony table. Susan momentarily sobered up. Were people staring at them as they rushed by? Did strangers know what she was planning?

"Where to?" Jeffrey asked as they neared his car.

Susan looked up at the bright moon.

"Somewhere dark."

He followed her gaze and stumbled backwards. She was suddenly determined to do *it* that night so pulled him upright.

"We can go to my room."

"I'm not allowed. We'll get in trouble."

"Not if we're quiet."

She was certain others had done it at the quarters, she'd heard them grunting through the walls.

Jeffrey drove slowly, not wanting to be pulled over by the police. The drink cleared his vision, made the traffic lights brighter, red to orange to green but they might not believe that. He concentrated on keeping the car in line with the white road markings.

"Left here."

They bumped off the kerb.

"Don't park too close. Go down there, in front of that motorcycle. They spot cars that are parked all night."

Susan put her finger to her lips before they crept up the path. She was always slightly ahead, beckoning to Jeffrey when she knew the way was clear. It only took a few minutes but when she closed her bedroom door they were both out of breath. Adrenaline rushed through them, pushing aside the wobbliness of the wine feeling.

Jeffrey scanned the room. There was nothing to personalise it apart from some cheap bottles on the dresser. There were no photos, no pictures on the walls, no pink fluffy bears on the bed like he thought girls usually had. He sat down and patted the empty spot next to him. Susan obliged. He kissed her whilst rubbing his hand in circles on her left breast. She was aware of each movement and waited to feel aroused. He moved his hand over to her right breast. She thought it odd, dull. Her bra started to rub uncomfortably against her skin. When he moved his hand further down the mechanics continued. She gave up expecting to feel passion, had always suspected it was a myth. When he entered her she flinched at the pain but was glad it was done. After a few raw minutes he rolled to the side, kissed her cheek, closed his eyes. His skin stank of sweat and booze. She lay on her back on a third of the bed, not wanting to touch him. She was right. They'd all exaggerated the pleasure, the body was a tool, not a toy. Susan turned her head to study his face. He was semi-handsome, definitely not ugly, and he had a steady job, two parents, no siblings. It was unlikely anything better would come along. He would do.

"Wake up." She nudged him. "You have to go now." She pushed him harder. He snorted and coughed. "You have to go." She pushed him so hard he rocked back and forth then woke, startled. "You've got to go straight away or I'll get in trouble."

Jeffrey rolled to sitting and put on his trousers, socks and shoes. He hadn't taken off his underpants or shirt.

"Do you have any water?"

"No."

He checked for his keys. When he leant over to kiss her she turned her head away from him so he pecked her on the cheek.

"I don't know the way out."

He sounded like a toddler. Susan sighed then led him down the corridor, the stairs, the hall. They made it to the front door. She stood on the steps, bare feet sending goose bumps up her calves.

"I'm free tomorrow, I mean today. I've got the day off work," she said.

On Saturdays Jeffrey got up late then spent the afternoon at the pub. His mother cooked chicken pie for dinner followed by lemon cheesecake, his favourite, with white wine to accompany it.

"I'm busy today."

"Right." She pursed her lips.

"How about Tuesday evening?"

"Maybe."

He put his foot in the door, after all, they had just done it.

"Pick you up at seven?"

She nodded. He ran away. Susan slammed the front door, not caring who she woke. She stormed up to her room and banged that door shut before pacing back and forth, eventually plonking herself on the bed. A sticky mess clung onto her thigh. Disgusted, she pulled the sheets off and threw them in the bath. She scrubbed and rubbed until she was certain there was no evidence of what they'd just done and as she hung them up to dry she told herself to be pleased she was no longer a virgin. She was a woman, one who'd achieved her goal, lose your virginity by the fifth date, tick. In fact add a gold star as she'd reached her objective early.

The sheets were too long for the wardrobe door she'd hung them over. The bottom of them remained floppy in a puddle of water that had dripped onto the floor. She felt dirty like the sheets so had a bath. She exfoliated with a nailbrush then dried, dressed and waited until six thirty to eat breakfast. Two nurses were already in the kitchen, in uniform.

"I mean who has a bath at that time?"

"God knows. Maybe it was lovers trying something new."

They giggled.

"Christ's sake. I've got a double shift today and some idiot's pulling that."

"Think karma."

"What?"

"What goes around comes around. Karma says they're going to split up. Karma says there's now a baby in that belly."

"Sandra! You're terrible." Louise was wonderfully appalled at her friend's twisted wish. "Don't say that.

That's shocking, you shouldn't say that. You're awful!"

They laughed as they left the room, their dirty dishes stacked in the sink even though the sign clearly stated that they should wash them up and put them away. Susan was so innocuous they hadn't noticed her sitting near them. Susan who'd forgotten about contraception after drinking all that alcohol. But it had to be done right in the middle of a cycle for a baby to be made, she was sure she'd read that. She put Sandra and Louise's cereal bowls in the bin, underneath some of the food waste from the night before, washed and put away her dish and spoon, then got her nurse's diary from her bedside drawer and there was the circle, twenty two days ago, around number seventeen. She was safe. She picked up a pen and wrote in the rectangular box, blank apart from a thirteen in its top right hand corner, 'Jeffrey'. It didn't look important enough. She added 'date with' in front of his name. She had a date with Jeffrey Jeffreys on Tuesday 13th. Very good.

Calton

Cal returned to his house each daytime with Johnny by his side. He had the only set of keys which meant the boys had no fear of getting caught as they smoked their way through the week. Some days they invited a select few to join them: Mark, Jordan and his friend Frank who'd bring his records, teaching Cal about the ones that were good and the ones that weren't, the whys and why nots of music, until their weed tin had only half a teaspoon of dust left in its dented corner.

~

Johnny grabbed his car keys off the bedside cabinet.

"Time to go shopping. We'll head up to the mountains then back to yours."

"I've got no cash."

"What?"

"We spent the last of it on the burgers. I've only got a few dollars left."

"Aww shit. My allowance isn't due for another two weeks. How are we going to last until then? I thought you had loads."

Cal stared at his legs, tanned from mornings of surfing

followed by afternoons of smoking, no raw burn this year, his mother would be proud. He told Johnny to drive to Hargrave and Jonson's, the solicitor's in town.

"Wait here."

Johnny rested his head on the back of his seat. Half an hour later he woke with a start as Cal jumped into the passenger seat and tapped on the dashboard.

"To the mountains my good man."

He flicked fifty dollars at Johnny who whoop whooped as they headed out of town on the road to Nimbin to Gerry, to their dealer, to Gerry with a G not a J man.

~

Three weeks later, they'd finished that batch.

"I've got a plan," said Johnny.

"Yeah?"

What Cal liked most about being stoned was that the sofa, chair, bed, the floor, they were always the most comfortable they'd ever been. And he hadn't thought of his mum and dad hardly at all, even when he was lying in their living room, sprawled over their furniture. Grieving was easier that way, when you couldn't feel anything.

"Gerry said if we shift a package for him, just up to Noosa and give his mate a lift back, he'd give us a stash in return."

"I'll get more money." Cal raised his hand to block his friend's idea.

"You shouldn't be spending so much on weed. And you can't go asking for more so soon, the adults'll get suspicious. This'll be fun, an adventure."

"I dunno. He's a bit weird, don't you think?"

"There's no risk. I've said we'll go in the morning and—"

"Jesus Johnny."

"It's safe, I promise. He'd go himself only he's bust his leg. He had a bandage on it and everything. We'll take the boards as if we're making a day of it and if anyone asks we'll just say we're going surfing and getting you new shorts and that's it. It'll be a laugh, a change to hanging out in this shithole, no offence."

Cal waved away the apology.

~

Gerry's house was at the end of a mile long dirt track, surrounded by tall grass, some of which had been flattened to offer a route to the wooden steps that led to the porch where a wasted man was lying in the shade on an old green sofa.

God knows how many snakes were snoozing in the long grass, thought Cal as he pulled his feet up onto the car seat. Everyone knew they could slither through the tiniest of spaces into cars, under beds, over sleeping bodies. That obviously didn't worry the comatose Gerry. Cal stayed in the car. Johnny tapped Gerry on the shoulder then shook his arm. Gerry jumped up making Johnny jump back, ready to run. Recognition was followed by relieved laughter, Gerry still giggling as they went inside.

Cal couldn't see any other cars though tyre tracks led round the back of the house. Gerry must have one, living so far from everywhere. Was he married? He didn't look married. Cal guessed he could have a girlfriend though his skin was so leathery and lined he must be pretty old and who would want to go out with that. An engine interrupted Cal's imaginings. He looked in the rear view mirror and saw a red car which came to a stop parallel to

Johnny's. A guy jumped out, looked briefly at Cal then ran up to the porch. Mike Taylor from the year above them in high school. Johnny came out of the front door just as Mike reached it. They ignored one another and Johnny ran to the car carrying a small cardboard box. He wrapped it up in a blanket, lodged it on the back seat, under their surf boards, then put a slip of paper on the dashboard.

"The address and directions for once we're off the highway."

Mike's car had left them no room to turn round so he started reversing up the track. Cal read the note.

"Is it thirty three or twenty three?"

"What?"

"I can't make it out."

"Give it here." Johnny took his feet off the pedals and checked the address. "Twenty three."

"Yeah? Are you sure? We don't want to go to the wrong house, not with something like this. There's a line underneath the—"

"It's twenty three, that's what he said. Honestly Cal, you're always looking for problems. Lighten the fuck up would you."

Johnny reversed round the corner onto the road and lit a cigarette before heading down the mountain.

~

Two and a half hours later they pulled up outside twenty three Edward Street. It was a road full of brand new brick houses rather than the clapboard ones that dominated Byron Bay. The lawns of all the houses were a bright, daily watered green and the pavements so clean it was as if they'd never been walked on. There was no dust in the air, no sand on the driveways from where the boots of cars had been opened and emptied. Metal shutters were pulled down over the two front windows of number twenty three. The red front door was closed.

"It looks shut up for the summer. I told you it was thirty three."

Johnny tapped on the steering wheel before reaching to the back seat and pushing the surf boards out of the way so he could pull out the package.

"Come to the door with me."

"Why?"

"This is for you as well as me," Johnny snapped as he got out of the car. "Don't be a dick. The least you can do is come with me."

Cal walked a few steps behind his friend. Once the two of them were on the terrace, Johnny knocked on the door.

"Hold on," a male voice called.

"Told you," mumbled Johnny.

A man who looked the same age as a grandad opened the door. His white golfing trousers were too tight over his belly, a pale blue top accentuating rather than covering up the flaw. His what should have been bald head was covered with a bleached blond toupee. He beamed at them.

"How can I help you lads?"

"You're alright," said Johnny. "I think we've got the wrong house. Sorry."

The guy clocked the package. "Selling something?"

"Nah," Johnny replied, turning round.

"A friend of Gerry's maybe?" the golf man grinned. "Why don't you come inside?"

"Who's that?" a lady's voice called from the back of the house.

"Just some boys raising money for the lifeguards darling."

"Oh that's nice," she said. "Be generous."

"When am I not?" he shouted. "She's such a caring soul," he said to Johnny and Cal. "This way boys."

The man opened a white door that led them off the hallway straight into the garage where he hoisted a cobalt blue leather golf bag out of the boot of his car. He emptied it of the clubs then reached deep inside it, pulling out a package a tenth of the size of theirs.

"I'll swap you that one for this one. How's about that then?"

Johnny held onto his more tightly. "I thought we were taking a friend of Gerry's back, not—"

"Oh," the man laughed. "This is Gerry's best friend, son. Don't you worry about that. Now I would offer you boys a drink but I'm teeing off in twenty minutes so you'd best get on your way. It's a long enough drive back to Byron. I take it that's where you're from, judging by the surf boards? I'm guessing that's where I can find you if Gerry doesn't get this eh?"

He led them out the way they'd come in so they didn't even get to see his Mrs.

"Honestly, it's the least I can do, please, take it all," he boomed. "Wonderful work you're doing boys. Just wonderful."

~

In return for the delivery of the golf man's package Gerry gave Johnny a bag of weed.

"If you want more you can do the same again next week."

"Thanks Gerry. We might well do."

"Does he speak?" Gerry pointed to Cal.

"Yeah, course."

"I've never heard him speak."

"He lost his mum and dad last month, within days of each other. He's traumatised."

"No shit?" Gerry studied Cal. "Hang on a sec." He went into the kitchen and got a powdered milk tin out of a cupboard, picking a white paper bag out of it. "Have these. They're stronger than the weed. You'll forget all the shit stuff man. I'm sorry to hear about your mum and dad. I mean, that's just so fucking sad."

Cal accepted the bag, too scared to say no or ask what was inside. "Thanks. Man."

"What did he give you?" Johnny asked in the car.

They looked inside and saw a stash of multi–coloured pills.

"I bet they're to help you sleep or something. Gerry's good like that. He knows exactly what sort of pill a person needs. He's like a doctor but better because he's more caring, more generous with his prescription. No-one knows more about drugs than he does. They're his life, his passion."

~

Johnny's mum caught them creeping up the stairs.

"Set the table would you Johnny. Did you get your shorts Cal? Let's see them. Was it busy?"

"They didn't have any in his size."

"What? In all of Brisbane? That's ridiculous."

"I know. Tell me about it. And after driving all that way. He complained in one shop didn't you Cal? I said to the assistant that wasn't the standard we expected when we came into the city."

"Good for you." She put a bowl of potato salad on the table. "Call your sister down would you. She's been in her room all day swooning over that Elvis bloody Presley. Fine chance she's got of making him her husband. Cal love, are you hungry? Would you like peas as well as sweetcorn? Help yourself to whatever you like darling. Try and eat a bit for me."

"Will do. Thanks Mrs Irving. I'll just go and wash my hands."

He hid the rainbow coloured pills under his mattress. Johnny put the weed under his.

"Just for tonight," he said. "Then we'll keep it at yours."

As Cal nodded a shadow ran past the door.

"Was that Ann?"

"Better not have been."

They hurried down the corridor and found Johnny's sister already sitting at the table, helping herself to a chicken wing.

"Were you spying on us?" Johnny muttered.

"As if," she sneered. "Why would I want to do that? Smelly bastards."

"Oi." Her mum clipped her ear. "Language missy."

~

"Mum, I've got belly ache. It's really bad."

Ann held onto her stomach and leant forwards.

"That's not fair. She's making it up to get out of doing the dishes."

"Shush Johnny. You don't know what it's like to be a woman. You don't understand what we go through. Do you want to have a lie-down honey?"

Ann nodded, smirking at her brother as he and Cal

began to clear the table. She went straight to their room to check under Cal's bed, sure that her brother would make his mate risk getting caught with whatever they'd been out buying that afternoon. One hand held the thin mattress up while the other felt along the wire springs. "Bingo." She grabbed the bag and checked inside. Coloured chocolate sweeties. She put them in the pocket of her dress for later and was about to check Johnny's mattress when she heard Cal and Johnny's voices. She nipped out of their room, back into hers, diving into bed, lying with her back to the door. She held her breath. Johnny and Cal mumbled in their room. She got ready to jump up and defend herself in case they saw what was missing but they didn't burst in. She reached into her pocket and grabbed a handful of the sweets, shoving them all in her mouth so there was no way they could ask for them back. She sucked and swallowed a few. They tasted different to Smarties. She chewed the ones left in her mouth but instead of chocolate a bitter taste spread over her tongue, texture like powder. Part of the coloured casing fell on her sheet, marking it blue. Her mum would go crazy, they were the new ones she'd chosen for her birthday. She couldn't spit the gunk out and make more of a mess so she grabbed the water by her bed, drinking fast to get rid of the sludge in her mouth then she ran to the bathroom and brushed her teeth. The taste was sharp and disgusting like medicine. Drugs. They were illegal bloody drugs, the naughty bastards. She knew her brother smoked weed like the hippies that hung out near the Pass. She'd smelt it when she saw him and his mates at the beach that time even though he'd denied it and threatened to punch her if she dared mention anything to their mum and dad. She'd show him now, make him wonder where the bag had gone, insist on having money from him if he wanted the rest back. And she'd get high. She was fourteen. That was old enough, time for new experiences. She filled her water glass and downed another nine tablets. She may not have kissed a boy yet but wait until she told Frances and Carina that she'd got as high as a kite like the big kids. They'd think she was awesome. She sat on the bed waiting for the weirdness to hit her. Her eyelids went droopy. She'd have a little nap then tell Johnny she'd found his stash and tested it, and he'd better give her five dollars if he wanted the rest back, or ten dollars maybe. That'd show him.

~

"Are you going to take one?"

"Nah."

"Why not?"

Cal shrugged as he pulled off his T-shirt.

"They might be nice. I'd have one if I was you."

"You want one, is that it?"

"No."

"You can have one if you like," said Cal. Johnny always wanted to try anything Gerry offered, and he'd missed having his smoke that night. "I know you want one, don't lie about it. You can have all of them. I don't want them. Just say so."

"I don't. I'm fine. I don't need that sort of shit anyway. I prefer a spliff. It's mellower."

Johnny paced the room, twitchy without his evening constitutional. He turned the light off and rolled from side to side, unable to get comfortable.

~

"Straight to yours after breakfast?"

"Yeah." Cal felt with his fingers under his bed. "Where are they? Have you taken them already?"

"Ha-ha. Very funny."

"Seriously." Cal lifted the mattress onto its side. They could see straight through the gaps in the wire to the floor.

Johnny pulled the mattress right off the bed.

"Ann," he said. "I'll bloody kill her." He burst into her room. "Ann you little shit. Did you take the stuff from under the bed?" He prodded her. "Answer me. You did, didn't you?" He shoved her shoulder. She rolled onto her back, a dribble of spit hanging from the side of her mouth. "Shit. Shit." He rolled her onto her side again. The packet of pills fell off the bed and onto the floor, a few of them scattering over the floorboards. He scooped them up, grabbed the bag and counted. There were only eleven left and Cal had said there were thirty three. "Ann, wake up you bugger. Stop messing with me."

Cal ran down the hall to fetch Mr and Mrs Irving.

~

They pumped her stomach in the hospital. They put a line in her arm to hydrate her, another to keep her asleep.

"You're sure she's stable?"

"Yes." The nurse rested her hand on Ann's mum's arm. "Why don't you get some air? You've not moved for five hours."

"I don't want to. I can't leave her."

Susan

The soreness and stinging when peeing had gone. Susan slipped on her navy dress, the only one Jeffrey hadn't seen. Rachel had pushed a note under her door asking for the silver shoes back. Susan's reply stated, 'Wednesday.' She transformed her lips to a sultry red and waited.

He didn't arrive at seven o'clock, the agreed time. She'd never understood how someone could know they had to be somewhere at a certain hour yet only leave with enough time to arrive late. At quarter past seven Susan tapped her fingers on her thighs and wiggled her toes in the uncomfortable shoes. At twenty five minutes past seven she cursed his slovenly attitude. At eight minutes to eight o'clock there was a knock on her door.

"Date's here," the anonymous voice called. Susan's frown lines deepened.

He was sitting on the steps, chatting to three nurses, a cigarette held casually in his right hand. She tapped her fingertips together whilst waiting for him to notice her. Jeffrey's nattering made him more confident, the expectation of his date had coated him with a childish swagger. He could be witty when in the mood. See.

"Here she is! Good evening darling," he slurred.

The beige tights made her skin tone insipid but he liked where those shapely legs led. He tipped his head. She tilted hers upwards disapproving of his flirting with those girls. He held out his hand and the bystanders stared. Susan walked right past him. He threw down his cigarette and scampered after her.

"Where are we going?" she asked.

"Where would you like to go?"

"You're late."

"Sorry. I—"

"What have you planned?"

"Would you like to see a movie?"

"What's on?"

"I'm not sure."

"And you don't even have the decency to apologise. Who raised you?"

Jeffrey felt blue all of a sudden. His earlier nonchalance scarpered. Susan forced herself to smile at him. Be. Nice. Susan.

"A movie sounds lovely."

Jeffrey concentrated on the road. He slipped his left arm down by the handbrake and took out his flask.

"There's a dance at The Bellview on Saturday. Would you like to go?"

He wasn't sure he wanted to go with her but what if he never found anyone else? He'd bedded her and she was decent looking, better than decent. She'd do. She was better than nothing.

Susan had never been to The Bellview. Her initial reaction was to say no because she didn't know how to dance and didn't like the noise of music but if she was to escape the other nurses, the drunken flailing and wailing, the tears and tantrums, the shallow chats, the nonsense of communal living…

"Alright then."

The movie was dull, the humour childish. Susan didn't understand why everyone around her kept laughing so loudly. She'd refused Jeffrey's offer of popcorn, couldn't bear the thought of money being wasted on a food with no nutritional value. He didn't buy any for himself but did sneak in one of his hip flasks. Each time he offered her a swig she refused, imagining his germ filled saliva dribbling down the silver neck, floating in the alcohol. She moved her hand to her nose to cover the smell of cheap perfume, his whiskey breath and too many bodies too close together.

The couple sitting next to her started to kiss. Susan was glad it was her beside them, not Jeffrey. She didn't want him thinking she'd act in the same way, not in public. Her eyes kept darting right. The boy's hand slipped under the girl's dress and the girl pushed her thigh down on his wrist. Susan stared, fascinated. When their lower bodies stopped gyrating she looked up.

"Pervert," said the writher, poking her tongue out before pushing her boyfriend towards the aisle. Three girls behind them spotted the row and wished they'd taken more notice of what was going on until laughter echoed round the room pulling their fickle attention back to the screen.

"Stupid girl," spat Susan. Her cold stare stopped Jeffrey from asking what had happened. He took another swig of whiskey. To his surprise she held out her hand for the flask and took four quick swallows. The smell reminded her of the disinfectant they used in the wards. It warmed her stomach.

By the end of the film they'd drunk every drop. Susan floundered on leaving the cinema. The world had tilted by twenty five degrees. She looked around to see if anyone else had noticed, thought of the boy's hand under the girl's skirt, turned to Jeffrey and kissed him hard on the lips.

"Yours?" he asked.

"Not on a week day."

He pouted. She tipped her head to the back of the car.

"You're sure?"

She took the flask from inside his jacket pocket and swallowed air.

"I've got more." He squeezed his hand under the seat and pulled out one of his back-ups.

~

Susan woke still wearing her dress from the night before, with a sore head and red rashes on both knees. She lay very still. Moving made the pain worse. There was no light in the room. Her curtains were heavy, the one decent thing she'd brought from her old home.

She pictured her mother, father, sister. No natural conversation was found. She despised them all. When she left home, she'd promised herself she'd keep moving forward, always in control, but now she was weak with Jeffrey's alcohol still in her blood. She spied on her mother as she moved round the house, wiped off fingerprints wherever she found them: dare they touch the table, dare they leave a streak on the banister, dare they breathe on the mirror in the hall. That had been a bad day. It wasn't her who'd marked it with pink pen but it was her who'd accidentally knocked it off the screws when proclaiming her innocence, causing it to smash into hundreds of pieces that raced to every corner of the room. She'd been made to pick up each shard: no brush, no pan, no sweeper. She'd crawled on her hands and knees, tiny daggers slicing her skin where she couldn't see the glass. Hours later she was allowed to go upstairs where she took a pair of tweezers from the bathroom cupboard and sat on the floor patiently plucking the glass from her skin. Until her mother caught her and grabbed them off her.

"I'll have to disinfect these now you selfish idiot. Christ, I could kill you some days. Do you exist purposefully to infuriate me?" She pulled her daughter by the elbow to standing, knowing just where to squeeze on the joint so the pain made Susan twist to the right, trying to get away but not actually daring to, keeping her head away from her angry mother. Susan made no noise, not even a whimper. "I hope you've learnt your lesson, destroying our things. That cost a lot of money that mirror. It meant the world to me. Go on, get out. Go. Your presence destroys me!" she screamed as she threw her daughter out of the door, onto the floor of the landing. Susan heard the key turn in the lock as she crawled as quietly as she could to her room. Then she heard her mother sobbing.

~

Susan banged her fist on Rachel's door, on the space next to the sparkly pink star with a capital R in its centre.

"I wondered where they'd got to," exclaimed Rachel.

"I left a note. Why were you wondering? Did you not understand it?"

Rachel took the shoes from Susan and stepped back

into her pink boudoir. The fuchsia eiderdown was covered in so many silk cushions there was no room to sleep. A shaggy sheepskin rug lay on the pale grey linoleum floor. A full length mirror stood in the corner of the room, squeezed between the dresser and desk, draped in scarves that were all colours of the rainbow. The desk was covered in the make-up that wouldn't fit on the dresser: lipsticks, powder puffs, eye creams and nine bottles of perfume. Where did she get the money for so much nonsense?

Rachel put the shoes next to another six pairs that were lined up beneath the window ledge, the only sense of order in the room, then she jumped on the bed, grabbed a cushion to hug.

"Well?"

"I'm sorry, I—"

"No! Never mind the shoes. How's it going? What's he like? I'm assuming you've seen him again, hence..." and she pointed to the sparkling silver pair. "Is it love?"

Susan was wary of being talked about in the kitchen or the canteen at the hospital.

"It'll do."

Rachel let out a mock scream of frustration and threw a cushion at her. Susan ducked and curled to protect her head, ready to take the hit then run. But no hurt came. There was no battering on her scalp or shoulders. She let her hands drop down. Rachel was staring at her, confused and embarrassed. Susan added shame to the mix and ran out of the room.

"Susan!"

She locked her bedroom door and curled up in the corner.

~

"You think that hurt. Well? Do you?"

Her mother was furious, so full of rage she flung Susan from wall to door to wall not caring about her cries. "Answer me."

"Yes."

"Nothing. That was nothing compared to what I can do to you, you little shit."

She grabbed her daughter by the collar, pushed her hard against the wall then swung her back onto the floor. The girl was so skilled at falling she didn't crack her head.

"That's only the start, do you understand me?"

The little girl covered her head with her hands as the mother grabbed her jumper at the back and pulled her up. She moved hands to arms, squeezed and shook.

"Why do you make me so mad? Why couldn't you do as I asked?"

"Sorry."

"What?"

"I'm sorry," she cried.

"Too late stupid child. You always get it wrong. You're always too late and so infuriatingly stupid."

The mother squeezed so tightly there'd be five marks on each arm in the morning. Then she shoved the girl away so violently she cracked her wrist on the mantelpiece as she fell onto her side.

"Damn you to hell and back. Why do you make me do this?"

She kicked the heel of her daughter's foot, hard.

The little sister hardly dared breath in her bedroom. The father sighed and continued to read his newspaper, telling himself that all houses were the same, this is how children were raised and anyway, she was an odd child, even if she was his own flesh and blood and he shouldn't really think like that. Alice was so much easier to love whereas Susan, there was something not quite right about her.

~

Susan's cheeks reddened as she remembered ducking. She'd ignore Rachel from now on. A problem ignored was a problem solved. And she'd catch Jeffrey for good though she'd made a mistake in agreeing to go to The Bellview. There was no way she could learn to dance by Saturday and now she had no sparkling shoes to distract from her stiff legs. At least he was a drinker. She'd just have to encourage him to drink more than usual and then he wouldn't notice.

Susan

Jeffrey loosened his collar. He'd filled four flasks that were now strategically placed throughout the car. An extra one was in his cream jacket pocket.

"Can you knock on Susan's door for me? Thanks doll."

The girl winked. "Sure thing lover boy."

He liked the nurse's uniform, not the headpiece as that was too like the nuns at his junior school but the skirt, the tights, the way the thick belt showed where the waist was. Maybe Susan would wear hers for him one day.

Rachel hurried to Susan's room.

"He's here. So cute. You look fabby together." Susan stepped out of her room and closed the door behind her. "Do you want to borrow some shoes? Susan? Hey! I asked you a question. There's no need to be rude you know!"

Susan plodded down the steps in her flat, orangey brown leather lace ups. Jeffrey held out his flask. She drank and kept it on her lap or by her lips or put it to his lips throughout the journey so that by the time they walked up the path to the dance hall Jeffrey was on fine form. He held the door open with a flourish for his lady. The corridor they passed through was like the ones at the hospital, dull and non-descript, scruffy at the edges. The cloakroom was dingy. Susan was glad she didn't own an expensive coat; the girl handing out tickets looked shifty and no doubt at least one garment would be lost before the music stopped later that evening.

She blinked hard three times. Her eyes adjusted to the green, red and blue lights that flew over the ceiling, walls and air. Her skin changed colour according to the shade that briefly coated her before being whisked away to another soul. The music was so loud she couldn't hear Jeffrey. She drank to hide how dowdy she felt compared to the jewelled dresses that glided and bopped across the floor. It put her in a bad mood. She did not want what she looked like to matter to her. Jeffrey didn't hold his hand out and Susan was glad because she didn't know what to do with the sounds. There was no natural toe tap pumping through her veins. In weaker moments she envied the other girls but as the room tilted and Jeffrey helped her balance she was glad for what she had, though not utterly thankful because he was lucky to meet her too. She kissed him like the girl in the film poster near the bus stop. The music covered his groan.

"Shall we dance?" he asked.

Susan shook her head and pushed her lips against his neck, believing that was what he wanted, what she needed to do to make him hers. His knees buckled. This time she helped him stay upright.

"What now then?" Though he meant to look at her, his drunken eyes couldn't manage it.

"We should get married," she said.

He smiled. Susan wasn't sure if he'd heard her or not. He kept smiling though. Susan rotated her hips clockwise on his pelvis. She'd seen it so many times coming home from night shifts that she got it right first time.

"We could get married," she said again.

This time his eyes were closed when he smiled.

"Ha. Yeah. Right."

"Really?"

"Yeah."

"When?"

"What?"

She took the flask from his right hand.

"We need to celebrate, to tell someone. That'll make it feel real. Shall we tell your parents?"

He collapsed at the waist. When she lowered her head to his level she saw he was laughing. Tears streamed down his face at the ridiculousness of it all. Outraged, Susan stormed off. Jeffrey ran after her, grabbed her hand and led her from the hall shouting, "We're getting married! We're getting married!" Various faces smiled and unrecognisable voices congratulated them. Some looked on with envy, others with disdain seeing the glazed eyes, hearing the blatant slur in the speech of the groom to be.

"Smile."

A camera flashed. Susan's eyes turned red.

"How much?" shouted Jeffrey.

"As it's such a special occasion we can do a deal. How wonderful to capture it, the most important night of your life bar the wedding of course," the photographer laughed. He flapped the photograph back and forth. "It's called a polaroid. And considering the magic of it not that expensive, worth it for your beautiful bride to be eh?"

Jeffrey pulled his wallet from his pocket and fumbled through the notes.

"We want change," said Susan.

The photographer turned to Jeffrey. "You've got a strict

one there. Eagle eyed." Susan snatched the photograph from his hand. "Congratulations," the photographer called after them, sure it would all end in tears. She was a harsh one and him a drunkard, he could tell by looking.

When they reached fresh air Jeffrey raised his arms as he hollered to the dark sky. Susan crossed her fingers that her plan would work and Jeffrey wouldn't go back on his promise.

"Let's go there now, straight away."

He fell to the ground.

"Aww no." He closed his eyes and burped repeatedly, holding the top of his chest as if that would help him.

"Come on."

"Where?"

"To tell your parents. And no need for you to find me another room now as we'll soon be living together."

Jeffrey looked from her calves, over her thighs and chest until his neck ached from tipping back to see her face. He was struck by the full force of her will and fell on one arm. Using that hand to push himself up he lurched towards the car shouting.

"We shall! Let's go! Let's bloody well go. Come on then!"

Susan closed her eyes as they swerved round the corners.

~

"Momsi! Popsi! We're home!" He switched the hall lights on. "Wakey wakey guys! Momsi! Popsi!"

Susan immediately hated his terms of endearment. She was tired now, knew the meeting would go badly and needed either another drink or to be elsewhere. Her arm rested on the marble mantelpiece that was crowded with silver photo frames of the beloved son and his doting parents. Susan's elbow knocked over a square frame which tipped another two onto their backs. She was fumbling to stand them back up when Jeffrey introduced her.

"I'd like you to meet Susan."

Jane and John Jeffreys weren't sure whether to be angry or bemused, having been asleep for over an hour. They were used to hearing their son come in late and the mother often cleared up the mess he left early on weekend mornings, before her husband got up. Once, she'd missed a little pool of sick still on the floor. "Damned cat," John had admonished, whacking its bum with the back of his newspaper when he passed it. Jeffrey had never purposefully woken them up before. The girl started to say hello but was interrupted by their boy.

"We're getting married."

Jane laughed at the big joke. Then she saw Jeffrey's frown turn into his determined face, the one she'd watched since he was three years old, trying to learn a magic coin trick. He'd refused to give up, to wait until he was 6 + as the box had suggested so they'd pretended to him he'd mastered it in order to save a scene and get him to bed. She cut her chuckle short. All four of them stood in silence. Susan studied the polished wooden floors. She could see faces in the wood, distorted tree people pleading to be set free, not trodden on again. Why had they been flattened?

"Susan."

The floor rippled. The room span. Susan focused on the outstretched palm and managed to make her right hand reach it.

"Mr Jefflees."

After she'd shaken hands with him, she held her palm out to Jeffrey's mother.

"We can lunch when you're sober."

Jane Jeffreys turned on the balls of her feet and left the room.

"It's nice to meet you," said the father.

"Nice to meet you too," said Susan. If she concentrated really hard the words came out better.

"Why don't I drive you home?"

"I can drive."

"I don't think that's wise Jeffrey, not after a drink or two. I'll get dressed. Just give me a minute."

"Next Saturday we'll choose the ring," the groom-to-be promised his bride.

He had no savings but could borrow from his parents. They'd come round. It'd sort itself out. He kissed Susan, not noticing the urgent talks going on above their heads whereas she could make out most of the words. Years of a breath held too long and the absolute focus of every sense on whether or not her mother was approaching, what she was saying and if so, what mood was she in, had given her the finest hearing of anyone she'd ever met. In a busy ward she could pick out one set of footsteps in a dozen and tell the patient their consultant would be arriving in two minutes. When crossing a road she knew to stop for the car nobody else could see because it was twenty yards round the bend. When she stood in the kitchen she could tell which nurse's boyfriend's car had pulled up from the clunk of the door shutting and the way his footsteps made a crunch as he strutted up the driveway. And she was always right. Always.

The car smelt of fake strawberries from the paper air freshener stuck on the dashboard. Susan opened the window half way. She could only help Jeffrey's dad with directions once they were nearer her quarters. She'd never been to their side of town before with its large houses and solid oak floors.

"I'll watch to see you're inside safely."

Once the front door was closed, Susan heard him accelerate away. She felt vaguely ashamed so swallowed a pink pill to ward off bad dreams and before it took effect realised she and Jeffrey hadn't arranged their next date. She fought the fog but her timing was all wrong. She would have to sleep and sort it out tomorrow.

~

On Sunday afternoon Susan saw Jeffrey's car through the kitchen window. She returned to her room and waited for the knock on her door.

"Visitor."

Susan checked that her hair was sitting neatly on her peaky face. Her stomach churned from hunger or hangover, she wasn't sure which. Jeffrey was sitting quietly at the top of the steps, not speaking to the girl next to him who was seeking a last drag from her fag. The smoker watched them and decided not to stay. Susan smelt last night's alcohol on him. The least he could have done was showered.

"You got home alright?"

"Obviously."

He paused. "They told me to call it off."

"Ah."

"I said no." She raised an eyebrow. "Next Saturday we'll shop for a ring then have lunch with them. You need to get to know each other, that's all." He mistook her anger for nerves. "They'll be fine. They just have to get used to you."

It was the first time Jeffrey had rebelled. Subjects he'd studied at school were what his father had recommended, his job was one his mother's best friend's husband had found for him. But getting engaged to a girl they'd never met before, that was all his idea. Susan called his bluff.

"When?"

"Saturday."

"No. When will we get married?"

"I don't know," he faltered.

"Soon?"

"Next year sometime."

"No. This month." He looked incredulous. "Or next month. We can compromise with next month."

He agreed, not thinking about what it really meant. It was after midday and the thirst was upon him.

~

Jane sat facing the fireplace, ready to pounce. John stood. His left knee buckled occasionally as he tried to lighten the mood with a tale from work about the Christmas party the year before last. Susan sat on the floral sofa next to Jeffrey. She was cross because she'd behaved as politely as she knew how. She'd smiled at her fiancé's dire jokes and not commented when his mother didn't congratulate them or admire her ring, though Susan noticed she'd hugged her son warmly, grasped and held him tightly in front of the undesirable bride-to-be. And now as they sat awkwardly it struck Susan how useless Jeffrey would be with his parents living so close. Rather than make polite

85

conversation she planned a move, worked out the value of her savings now the first of two expected inheritance cheques had arrived from the solicitor, plus the wedding gifts they might receive. Would the mother balk if they asked for money instead of a toaster that perfectly browned slices of bread Susan could never enjoy? Of course she would.

"I should go." All three of them focused on her. "I'm on an early shift tomorrow, twelve hours, double time. Do you work Jane?"

"No."

"I didn't think so."

John was relieved his wife didn't rise to the bait, thinking only of the here and now rather than the number of similar afternoons he'd have to endure if the marriage went ahead.

When Jeffrey returned from dropping Susan home he didn't tell them his fiancée wanted to move to another town so he and she could truly be alone and together for the beginning of their married life. He didn't intervene in the first shouting row he'd ever seen his parents have. And when his mother started to cry, he went upstairs and shut the door to his bedroom rather than hug her like he usually would have done if he'd seen her so upset.

That was when Jane knew she'd lost him to that strange, cold girl. After all those years of nurturing and loving, he was gone. She wept all evening and through to the morning when she wiped her eyes before waking Jeffrey, agreeing to go along with what she believed was a complete and utter sham.

"It'll end in tears and never last," she warned both her son and her husband as she served them breakfast.

Calton

Tom Irving paced the hospital's corridor, cigarette in hand, unsure whether he wanted to cry or hit someone. Both. He wanted to do both. He should have been better at looking after his little girl. The doctor waved him into the room. He put his cigarette out in the silver hip height ash-tray and as he stood behind his wife he couldn't look at Ann lying unconscious, needles in her arms. Instead, he focused on the doctor.

"She's stable now though the next twenty four hours are crucial. We're hoping there's no kidney damage and—"

Mr Irving punched the top of the pale green cushioned chair, making his wife moan.

"The good thing is we had the pills and know what most of them are. That helped a lot. This time tomorrow I'm hoping to be able to tell you she's on her way to a full recovery."

Mrs Irving tried to smile at him. Thank heavens for the clever doctors. She wanted them to know how grateful she was but couldn't talk without crying and the words that came out when she tried made no sense anyway.

"So what were the pills Doc? Medicines or hippy shit? I've read about that stuff in the papers. Is that what they were?"

"Mainly medicines. Someone Ann knows must have had a prescription they weren't using. It happens sometimes. Young people take them from their grandparents cupboards not realising how dangerous they are."

"She wouldn't have done that. And all our parents are dead. Where else could she have got them?" He clenched his fists to control the urge to punch. "I'm going to head home hon, just for an hour or two. Do you need me to bring back anything?"

"Tom, don't."

"What?"

The doctor left the room so they could have a private moment.

"It was an accident. And the doctor's sure she'll be fine. Please. Don't."

"We've a right to know where she got them from."

~

Mr Irving stormed through the pub as he shouted Johnny and Cal's names but no-one had seen them all day. He raced to Cal's house but that was empty too. And shabby, the garden not touched in weeks, dog shit on the pavement in front of it. Elizabeth would have cleaned that up in a jiffy. It looked sad, the house looked sad. He slowed down, the thoughts in his head too heavy.

~

Unable to find them, defeated, Mr Irving parked his car in the hospital car park. The boys were standing by the window inside his baby girl's room.

"Where have you two been?"

"Here," said Johnny, his eyes wide, terrified.

"I've been looking for you."

"They were mine," said Cal. "I'm sorry."

Mrs Irving started to cry.

"We took you in," said Tom through gritted teeth. "You stupid, stupid boy."

"I know. I'm sorry."

"No," said Tom. "That's not good enough." Johnny stepped from left to right, unsure of what to say, how to make it better, if he too should confess or not. Not, judging by the look on his father's face. "You're to pack your stuff."

"Dad, no. He—"

"Shut up. If it wasn't for your parents Calton, I'd be calling the police, you do know that?"

"Yes Sir. Thank you."

Cal sped out of the room. Johnny caught up with him by the lifts.

"Thanks for not dobbing me in." Cal shrugged. "You can have the weed from under my bed as a gift. I mean if you could take it now, as soon as you get your stuff, before my dad finds it, I'd really appreciate it. He'll go mental otherwise. Where are you going to go? Back to yours?"

"I guess."

"I'll see you tomorrow then. And don't worry. They'll be alright once it's all calmed down a bit. Bloody Ann. So typical of her to create a drama out of—"

"She nearly died Johnny."

"She's alright. It'll be alright. Panic over. Tomorrow yeah? If not, the day after. I'll be clucking for a smoke by then."

~

As Cal walked to the pub, he stuck his thumbnail into his finger. The pain of the skin splitting distracted him from the jabbing ache in his chest as he remembered his mum and dad were gone and he had no-one to turn to, no-one to go home to and tell about the day, his side of it. There was no-one to stand up for or believe in him, no-one to hug him and say it's alright son, we're here and tomorrow will be better. He had to get life right totally on his own now. He had no family.

Cal packed his clothes and wash stuff, took the weed from under Johnny's bed, not wanting it as a gift, only to stop him getting into trouble. Johnny was right, his dad was bound to search the place.

~

Mr Jonson stood in front of Cal in the reception area of the solicitor's office. For the first time since Cal was seven, he didn't offer a handshake.

"I heard what happened. It's probably best you leave town for a bit Cal. We can't have you staying here, influencing the other kids, being a danger to them."

The receptionist stared disapprovingly at Cal as if she and Mr Jonson were so much better than him. Cal had that lump in his throat like when he realised his mum had definitely stopped breathing. The lump turned to flutters as if his heart had forgotten how to work properly, that it was meant to sit in his chest not his thorax. He took deep breaths, trying to calm the racing feeling.

"We'll sort you out with some money and work out what to do with the house then I'm seeing you onto the bus, you hear me?" Cal followed Mr Jonson into his office. "Your parents would be so disappointed in you."

On and on he went. His words swirled around Cal's head. Mr Jonson saw the boy taking no notice and thought it was sad how some youths turned bad so quickly, all strange and angry. They should know better and he was sorry but death wasn't an excuse for such miscreant behaviour.

"Where are you going to go?"

"I'm not sure. North? West maybe."

That's where he could get lost rather than up the coast where he might bump into familiar faces one day.

"How much cash have you got left from last week?" Cal shook his head. "You spent the whole lot already? Jesus Calton. You need to be more careful. There's not an endless supply you know, you're going to have to make it last. Close your eyes a minute."

Cal did as he was told and when he peeked, Mr Jonson was turning the numbers on a safe behind his chair.

"Right then. Sign here and you can have this to see you on your way. Do you want the house sold or rented out?"

"Sorry?"

"The house. Do you want it sold or rented out?"

"Just leave it."

"It'll rot if you just leave it. I'll rent it out, use the money to cover the upkeep and put any spare in the bank for you." His tone softened. "Then you'll always have a home to come back to. Things will calm down. They always do. And some time away from here will do you good. How about Sydney? Or Melbourne? One of those two. That's where I'd go if I was young."

"I—"

"I've got an old college friend in Melbourne who manages the Royal Botanic Gardens. He might be able to get you some work there. I'll write down his number and tell him you'll be calling, then you'd best go home and pack for a chunk of time away." Cal accepted the green index card and put the roll of money in his shorts pocket. "It'd be good to see you again Calton, once the dust's settled and you're acting more mature. You're to leave today though. We'll be checking on you."

~

As the lady next to him fell asleep, her chin drooped to the right. Cal stared out of the bus window. They passed through a town made up of eight buildings. It looked cosy inside their houses, the bits he could see through the windows. It must be nice having a bed to lie in, a kitchen to cook in, a person to hug you good night. He closed his eyes but rather than sleeping he listed in his head the people he was angry with and why: his mother for being taken, his father for choosing to go, Johnny for being a coward, Johnny's mum for immediately accepting that it was Cal who was bad when she should have known better, the dad for wanting him to blame, Gerry for making it happen, Gerry's old golfing mate for giving them his stuff and finally, himself for making a mess of it all. And Ann. He was cross with Ann and that Gerry had promised the pills would be a good thing but they'd turned out to be such a bad thing. And himself again. When he'd taken the blame he'd taken a risk that they'd all pity him and he'd been wrong to do that, so more fool him for being an idiot. He deserved what he got, it was only fair he moved on. And on and on. He would buy maps and keep going. He'd loop all the way around the country before maybe returning one day.

Susan

As Susan sat down on the bus she saw a girl on the seat in front of her, aged around thirteen, turn to the mother next to her and look at her with love, you couldn't mistake the feeling. After they'd smiled at one another the child rested her head on her mother's shoulder and the mother turned her head slightly to the right to kiss her daughter's hair. It was not a new gesture. It had clearly been played out before. They were physically and emotionally comfortable in each other's company, more than comfortable, they loved each other, truly.

Susan tried to imagine what that felt like. It looked like a nice emotion to have and the fact that she'd never experienced it made her kick the seat in front of her, hard. The girl's head jolted. She sat back upright.

"Apologies. I'm so sorry," said Susan. "I was moving my bag."

"Not to worry," said the mother. She and her daughter smiled at Susan, their perfection making her want to slap their faces. How dare they be so soft and mushy? That's not what the world was like. She'd soon discover that, the child, and then where would she be without her precious mother to look after her. Everyone had to grow up and leave home one day. She shouldn't be so reliant, so needy from the looks of her. Susan bet she cried when she fell over or if another girl said a mean word. The mother should be ashamed of herself, raising such a weak child. Pah. They were pathetic.

Susan banged the back of their seat with her leg as she got up for her stop, this time not apologising. With her left foot she squished the edge of the mother's shopping bag that was a quarter sticking out onto the aisle, hoping she'd caught a pear or nectarine beneath her brown leather sole. That'd teach them. Being soft and gooey was no use and never would be.

The milk bar was opposite the bus stop. Susan hadn't been to one before though she'd heard the nurses in the kitchen talk about the cost of a strawberry shake with ice-cream versus one without or getting the largest size to share. She couldn't comprehend why someone would spend that much money on milk when they could have a cold glass at home where there were less germs to be caught and spread as well as it being cheaper. She took a deep breath before crossing the road. She shook off the idiots on the bus and put on her pretend face that she'd practised in front of the mirror especially for greeting her mother-in-law.

Who wasn't there yet.

Susan sat in a booth near the entrance so fresh air could blast over her when the door was opened and closed. She waved away the approaching waitress then checked the menu. The cheapest drinks were the squashes but she needed to appear generous so she'd go for an ice cream soda which was less than the cost of their fancy sundaes. The fourth time the bell over the door rang she saw Jane scan the room.

"Over here," Susan waved. "Your dress is lovely. Is it new? It suits you."

It was too tight. Susan wondered if it had ever fitted. She doubted it, could tell Jane was one of those in denial people who bought things the size they were ten years ago no matter that they'd eaten more and walked less ever since then. The heat of the day made small sweat patches peek out from under her arms, baby pink being the wrong colour for heat and the hiding of a maturer lady's hot flushing years.

Jane put her green leather handbag to the side of the seat and slipped awkwardly into the booth. Her thighs caught under the metal table. A waitress stood at the end of their booth, her hair coiffed in the same style as the other staff, her uniform prettier than Susan's nursing one, maroon with brass buttons, her head piece the same starched white as Susan's nursing cap but smaller.

"Good afternoon ladies. What can I get you?"

"I'd like a lime ice cream soda please. Jane? It's my treat. Pick whatever you like."

The words felt obviously alien but Jane was more pre-occupied with the menu than seeing her future daughter-in-law squirm. Susan ordered herself to relax, be nice, smile as much as possible. It had to go well, that was what she needed.

"My goodness, if I'd have known that I wouldn't have eaten lunch," Jane joked, too late for it to be funny. And Susan just managed to refrain from joking back, well you could certainly do with missing a meal judging by your waistband. "An egg malted milk please darling."

The most expensive drink on the menu. Susan pushed her right heel hard onto her left foot to distract from her fury. It would be worth it. She had to keep calm and make the mother like her, not adore her, there was no need for that.

"What colour lipstick is that you're all wearing? Isn't it divine Susan? What brand is it darling?"

"Cyclax," said the waitress as she took their menus. "From their new colour creme range. I can't remember which one, sorry."

"Well I adore it. I shall buy one for myself though goodness knows I won't look as pretty as you, all of you in here all so gorgeous. I've a son you know. He works at the hospital. He's very handsome. Are you courting at present?"

"She's such a joker talking about my fiancé," Susan said to the waitress who was squirming in the middle of the double glare from both her customers.

"I'll put your order through."

"You don't wear make-up do you Susan? Why's that then?"

"I don't need it."

"You think? I always thought, me and my friends actually, we'd say that a lady who doesn't wear make-up isn't to be trusted. If she doesn't even look after herself, how can she be a good wife, a decent mother, able to look after another person, someone's darling son or her own child for that matter?"

"I look after myself perfectly well. I eat just enough food so as not to make me pudgy and walk when I can instead of getting lifts or buses. It's good for the heart. You should try it, you and John."

"We're fine as we are thank you. No need to—"

"And I look after my finances. Always have done since both my parents died when I was little."

Jane whimpered as she imagined not being there for little Jeffrey. That thought created a physical hurt in her heart. No wonder Susan came across as odd, she'd obviously had no parenting. Jane should be a good Christian, try to see some warmth in the woman, difficult as it was because there was something cold in place of her soul, she was sure of it.

"Who raised you?"

"An uncle. But he was mean. I did not like him."

"You've no siblings?"

"No. I'm an only child the same as Jeffrey. I think that's one of the reasons why we understand each other so well though I guess he has you so not so similar. He always talks about how wonderful you are."

"He said you met at the hospital. Wouldn't you rather catch yourself a doctor?"

"No."

"I thought all nurses wanted to marry doctors. They look so handsome in their white coats, so educated."

"Not me."

"No. Not you. It's funny that. Jeffrey never excelled at school though he had talents of course, just wasn't sure how best to direct them but he was never academic or that sporty. I'm not sure what his projected earnings are, compared to a surgeon say. He might not be quite who you think he is."

"I'm not marrying him for his money." Susan pressed her nails into her tights under the table to keep the lies coming. "We love each other very much. I feel so blessed that I've met him."

Jane studied Susan's face, not believing a word of it, unable to point out to her husband exactly why but she was always right when it came to these things. Why wouldn't he listen and more importantly, why wouldn't Jeffrey? The woman sitting opposite had bewitched her only child. Or drugged him. Maybe that was it. She'd stolen medicines from the hospital and was feeding them to him, moulding him into what she wanted. If Jane was a betting women she'd have put a hundred dollars on it.

The waitress broke the worry as she placed two drinks between them and a bill under the silver straw dispenser. Susan sucked on her drink, unable to let go of the anger that she should have ordered the cheapest item on the menu as she couldn't taste it anyway. Jane slurped hers, like mother like son. Susan's teeth ached at the coldness. Stupid milk bar.

"I've saved up enough for a deposit for an apartment, nearly. If Jeffrey's got savings too we can—"

"He's too young for that. He's only twenty for goodness sake. How old are you, if you don't mind me asking?"

"A lady should never divulge her age." That's what her mother used to say.

"You can when it's family."

"Alright then. You start. How old are you?"

"Fifty nine." Susan's eyes widened, like most did when Jane told them. "It took a long time to have him. We'd given up then one day, a miracle."

"I'm twenty five." A few years here or there wouldn't hurt anyone. "I know I look older. I think it's from being orphaned so young, having to look after myself in life though that made me strong and capable. And now it feels like it was all in preparation for when I met Jeffrey so I'm able to look after him."

Jane didn't want another woman looking after her son,

that was her job. She should be enough. Why couldn't she keep doing it? He was still a child, still her little baby.

"Where will you live?"

"We'll rent initially then buy when we're sure where we want to settle."

"What do you mean where?"

"Obviously we need to see what area makes us happiest. Near the hospital preferably because of my night shifts or maybe we'll move somewhere else, say if Jeffrey were to get a promotion."

"He won't want to live somewhere else."

"No? Well in that case we'll stay here, look for somewhere local."

Although Susan was smiling Jane didn't trust her. If John was there he'd say she was reading too much into everything, the girl was trying, why couldn't Jane want it to work, she'd mollycoddled that boy for too long, it was time she let him live his life and look at the savings the girl had. It's not like she was after their money.

~

"We got on so well," Susan told Jeffrey.

"Really? That's great."

"Isn't it? I'm sure if you ask now, they'll happily pay for the wedding." She pulled up her tights. "You owe me three dollars for the drinks. Your mother picked the most expensive item on the menu and if it wasn't for me courting you I'd never have met her so wouldn't have had to buy her a malted milk. And you can pay for dinner tonight. That's what a man does if he's getting married to a lady."

There had to be advantages to seeing him.

~

Susan's shift finished at the same time the mothers walked their children home from school. She stepped onto the road in order to overtake their too slow a pace walking. She did not want to be like them. She would not become one of them. Why would a person go through the trauma of turning from a child where they had no control over their life to an adult where they should have total control, only to get married and have it taken away from them? She'd noticed that some women wanted a man to lead them but didn't understand why. She would do the opposite. She'd use her marriage to create a future that was bearable and Jeffrey would do what she wanted rather than it being the other way round. Plus the maths was simple; two wages were better than one. It made sense. It had to.

~

Jeffrey put a mouthful of pie near his lower lip but not in his mouth then he sucked it up like the hoover the man had demonstrated in the department store though that was a continuous noise whereas Jeffrey had gaps in between his slurps. Gather the food on the fork, raise and suck. Gather, raise, suck. Raise and suck. Did he not notice how quiet Susan was, how her cutlery didn't make a sound on the plate, not even the knife's tip on the china after it had cut through the meat and even that tap was so minimal it wouldn't disturb anyone. Gravy dribbled down Jeffrey's chin. Rather than grabbing a serviette to wipe it off, he left it. Did he have no feeling on that skin? Was he a total retard? She imagined the gravy covering his mouth and the end of his nose, somehow drowning the man while he sat at the table, such an innocuous weapon that no police officer or judge would believe there'd been foul play. Death by gravy would be the noisy man's sentence. And once he was dead on the floor there would be peace. Not a bad exchange Susan reckoned, his death for her peace. She smirked. That was a sacrifice she could live with.

Calton

When Cal opened his eyes there was a man sitting next to him. The stranger's legs were covered in a navy and grey pinstripe material. His shoes were black, once shiny but now scuffed, barely enough sole on each to stop dirt coating the balls of his feet. He looked straight ahead, ignoring Cal, a stale urine stink surrounding him, dirt in his hair, the skin on his fingers blackened from years of not enough washing.

"Are you lost?" Cal asked.

"No. Are you?"

Cal looked at him more carefully. Underneath his beige coat was a jacket that matched the trousers. It made no sense. That wasn't what people who slept in doorways usually wore.

"Why are you wearing a suit if you're not lost, if you don't mind me asking Sir?"

"Ah." The older man took a hip flask from his inside jacket pocket, unscrewed the lid and drank. "Therein lies a sad tale."

Cal waited but the storyteller was busy sipping. Cal closed his eyes. There'd been enough sadness. He would count to twenty then head to another spot where no-one would bother him.

"Seven years ago I arrived home to a policeman standing at my front door and he was kind but sad because my wife and sons had been killed in a car crash two hours earlier. After he left, uncomfortable because I'd refused his offer of calling my family, a neighbour, a friend, well then I stood in the hallway of my grand house with its five empty bedrooms, even a games room because I earned a lot of money back then, and I thought, what use is this house to me now. What use is anything and why on earth would I want possessions or a roof over my head when I haven't got Jean, Frank and Simon to share them with. I walked out of the house in the suit I was wearing. I kept walking. I had no feelings of hunger though a thirst got hold of me and the days trickled by and the miles flew past as I hitched lifts, finding out that strangers are more inclined to help a fellow in a suit though less so as I began to ripen. Gradually a pungent odour emanated from under my arms and feet, the crotch, my undergarments, no doubt you've noticed it and can smell it as I speak but are too polite to make it obvious as you're a well brought up boy. And that was all those years ago and here I am sitting next to you today, a place where you shouldn't be by the way. You need to stay away from the doorways. Because the fools and bastards, nasty bastards with foul souls, they can be drunker than you've ever been and run up with a well-aimed kick or piss upon your legs thinking it's hilarious, so go for the hidden spots where the selfish, bastardly badly raised ones can't see you. That's my advice and my years of experience make me worth a listen. As part of your instinct for self-preservation which I guarantee is in you somewhere, make sure you take heed of it."

"You've got a house?"

"Listen to me. I'm trying to help you."

"You own a house still somewhere?"

The man frowned at Cal. That wasn't what the young usually took from his story.

"I don't know. You try to help people and they just don't listen."

"Why are you on the streets if you've got a house?"

"I told you. And I doubt it's mine anymore anyway. It'll have been sold. My sister was one of those nightmare ones, always leeching from her little brother. She used to make such unsubtle comments about how lucky I was to have so much money – not luck, hard work. She cried about how little she had though she managed to spend an awful lot, and made unsubtle hints about how I could afford to give money towards her buying a bigger place as I was so lucky – not luck, hard work. She'll have sold the house as soon as she was legally allowed to and cried at my memorial service whilst counting up the dollars in her head."

He took a cigarette from Cal's proffered packet and Cal felt lucky he didn't have a sister waiting in the wings, desperate to grab his mum and dad's place.

"You," suit man pointed at Cal with anger in his voice. "You are young. You don't need people not looking you in the eye for the rest of your life, embarrassed by your presence on the street, you at their feet, them scuttling past you. You need to get a job, do something better."

"I don't mind."

"Well you should. For me it suits but you, you deserve not be invisible."

"My mum and dad died."

"So?"

"It was pretty shit actually."

"Of course it was. Better than losing a child though. Losing both boys, that was the worst thing a god, small g as far as I'm concerned, that was the worst thing he could have done to me. Are you religious?"

"I don't think so. You?"

"Not any more. Though it's in me. Once a Catholic, always full of guilt etcetera etcetera... I'd have jumped off a bridge if it wasn't for a fear of purgatory keeping me away from them forever, that nagging doubt, what if there is a heaven and a hell and an in between bit. Clever bastards. How can you afford a packet of those?"

"I brought a bit of money with me."

"You weren't too grief stricken then."

Cal's eyes widened.

"I'm just saying you had the foresight to think ahead so you don't really want to be destitute I reckon."

Cal stubbed his cigarette out on the pavement.

"Go and pay for a night in a hostel so you can shower and put clean clothes on, then go and get a job. You'll be amazed where being clean looking gets you. If you smile at people they'll smile back rather than look away, embarrassed. Your teeth are still good. You can be different to me and I'm aware it's not a competition but if it was, my grief would win. Your parents died first, that's the natural order of things. Stand up, walk away and don't ever sleep in a doorway again."

The suit man held onto Cal's shoulders as he rose and hobbled down the road, a stain on the back of his coat, old and ingrained, sadder than anything Cal had seen since his mother and father's bodies. The words that came from suit man's mouth did not match the impression he gave as people avoided him, didn't look at him, managed to swerve right or left in order to not see him. He was there but invisible. And he was right. Cal did not want to be that.

~

Cal called the number Mr Jonson had handed him and as a favour to an old friend, was given a job at the Botanic Gardens. Working outdoors was exactly what he needed rather than inside work where a person was surrounded by too many people in too close a proximity, no air to breathe, panic rising. Outside, the breeze blew away any moments of claustrophobia and shrouded him in an ability to exist in the world. It made his grief controllable.

That and the weed he bought from the other apprentice, Jack. Jack of all trades, Jack of the weed, Jack, do you need to blur the edges mate because I can help you? The all-knowing Jack who found him, his most regular client, a bunk in the young men's hostel he also stayed at, meaning there was hot water to shower in, cold water to drink, a kitchen to cook in. The staff turned a blind eye to the aroma that wafted over the tin roof as long as the residents were peaceful, which they were, much calmer than the boozing ones.

~

The wealthy ladies from St Kilda walked in heels that put their backs out, hair coiffured, lipstick matte. They all noticed the young gardener's cheekbones, his hands, his eyes, did you ever see such blue eyes as that boy has, the one who works in the gardens, a young fellow, new, very beautiful, the sort of face an artist would draw, a muse in any other era. How they saw his eyes when he was always looking down was through hard work on their part but they'd egg each other on to drop a tissue, a comb or a child's book out of a pram. He'd hear it, turn and pick it up, hold it out to them, all the clumsy ladies giggling like children as they accepted the return of their purposefully lost possession. Cal didn't understand them or what they were about though he felt self-conscious and knew something was up. He'd twist his lips unsurely at their grins and get back to work. If his mother was alive she'd have shooed the women off, protected him. He was too young for them for Christ's sake, she'd yell, get away from my beautiful darling.

Susan

Susan got dressed for her wedding in the nurses quarters. Her cardboard suitcase sat packed and buckled in the corner of her room, labelled Mrs J. Jeffreys. Several of the nurses who lived there had signed a card wishing her luck. In the weeks before the whirlwind wedding they'd seen her soften. Some of her anger was shed and they all gossiped amongst themselves about how it was a good thing, obviously the right path for her to follow. A few wished they too could be whisked down the aisle, others knew it wasn't for them. They were too young and the world was too big a place to explore, too exciting to be trapped with one man. But Susan was the hunter, not the game. Forsaking her maiden name meant freedom, from her family, from her past, to be known only as Mrs Jeffreys with whatever personality she chose to suit it best.

She drank three glasses of wine at the wedding meal, not enough to keep pace with her husband. He smiled at her as she finished her third glass, his cheeks glowing, a wide, mischievous grin making him look like a court fool. She smiled back, pleased that he was pleased. He offered her a fourth.

"Mrs Jeffreys."

He kissed her on the lips in front of everyone and because she was drunk, she let him. The fourth glass was downed in synchronised gulping. When he was pulled away to speak with a guest the strength of the alcohol hit her. The room became too hot. She couldn't see him among the bobbing heads so went to the corridor for some air.

There were other parties at the hotel. Guests staggered, laughed and ran down the carpet full of swirling reds and greens. She couldn't tell which belonged to their wedding party. She didn't know his family and friends well enough to recognise their faces. Apart from his mother and father, she'd met them all for the first time that day.

Leaning her right hand against the oak panels, she walked towards the open French doors at the end of the corridor. The smooth wood soothed her off balance mind, its solidity reassuring. The corridor was stifling. Smoke from cigarettes and cigars hung in a low mist, clinging to the walls, imitating the swirls in the carpet. She panicked, thinking the couple in front of her were whispering that it would be rude of her to go. Susan was not her own person now. She was married and should be with her husband. She turned through a doorway into the room they'd eaten in.

"Daughter-in-law!"

A large hug was bestowed upon her, oh the difference champagne made. Red feathers from the tasselled shawl tickled her cheeks and nose. Her arms were gripped too tightly to itch. Loose and lost feathers lay scattered over the floor, clues to the route her mother-in-law had taken. Jane's larger than her new daughter's frame was shown off in a tight navy silk dress, heels so high she'd leant forwards before the wine and they stopped her falling backwards after it. As the mother and her sister stared at her, Susan was aware she should say something, anything.

"Thank you for this. It's very generous of you."

"Oh hush." Tears welled up in Jane's over emotional eyes for the umpteenth time that day. "It's the least we could do. Jeffrey's our only son."

Jane's sobs got louder. The aunt comforted her.

"Mabel, I—" said Susan.

"Miriam," was the aunt's stern reply. "It's a shame you weren't free before the wedding. I so wanted to meet you before you both took your vows."

The aunt grabbed two more glasses of champagne from a passing tray and gave one to her tearful sister.

"Excuse me."

Susan left them to pick her to pieces.

~

Susan had persuaded Jeffrey that a week in the Blue Mountains was enough of a honeymoon for them both. She'd rather walk through the forests, scramble over giant rocks balanced on their tips as if ballerinas on pointe, than sit on a crowded beach in what amounted to underwear as men stared from behind their sunglasses at busts, bums, bellies, and smooth, hairless legs. It was tiring having to shave every few days now that she was with him. Once they were settled she'd stop and he could take her as she was born to be.

As she lay next to him on the third night she thought of what she'd learnt that she hadn't known before they got married. He made a slurping sound as he guzzled his morning tea, sucking up the liquid rather than putting his lips on the edge of the cup and quietly sipping. For all her superior airs and graces his mother had not done a good job of raising her son. Midday was his witching or was it twitching hour, where the first alcoholic drink of the day could officially be ordered because it was lunchtime not morning so that was alright then as far as he was concerned, what was her problem, stop judging me woman. There was his weakness and her knowledge. Knowledge was power.

There was never a day where he abstained from the drink and the tension generally left him after his third glass was emptied. By the fifth glass his eyes would stare at a point beyond his wife's head even though they were meant to be focused on her. *Over here* she'd think of calling, *look at me you fool, my eyes are this way, stop talking to the painting behind my chair you idiot.* That was the point where she hated him most, his inability to focus making her want to leave him but they were on honeymoon so she couldn't.

Now they were married she'd stopped drinking to keep up with him and he didn't seem to care. She'd thought it might make him temper his intake but no, he took it as permission to drink more: might as well finish the bottle, waste not want not, you go to bed, I'll be up in a minute, in an hour, three hours later stinking of booze and cigarettes, farting and burping like a bastard.

It wasn't meant to have soured so quickly. She knew she wasn't in love with him when she'd married him but she thought they'd be able to put up with each other for at least the first year, never mind the first week of their godly union. Perhaps the honeymoon part was the problem. It wasn't natural. They were spending too much unnatural time together. When they went home they'd both be working and out of the house for around forty per cent of the day, another thirty per cent for sleeping, leaving only around thirty per cent together, including meal times. She'd put up with worse. She could deal with that for as long as she needed to in order to get what she was due before moving on to the next thing. Susan was strong. She would manage.

~

When they returned home to their newly leased apartment, Susan ignored the here we are smile on Jeffrey's face. She turned her back on him and headed straight to the bedroom with her suitcase in order to sort out the laundry. Jeffrey had known not to suggest carrying her over the threshold. That knowledge made his shoulders heavy. He imagined gulping down a glass of white wine before pouring a second which he'd drink more slowly. In movies freshly married couples looked so happy. The bride squealed as the husband scooped her up in his arms, carried her into the house, rested her lovingly on the sofa or threw her down in a fun way and jumped on top of her ready to do the deed, hand past suspenders under a flared silk dress, into her undergarments. But Susan was in the kitchen pouring them both a glass of water, telling him to put his suitcase next to hers in the bedroom, not a hint of hanky panky.

"I'm going to head to the bottle shop before it closes. Would you like anything?"

"No."

He waited for her to ask what he was going to buy and

why wasn't she enough for him but instead she pushed past him into the bathroom. He was sure she disapproved of the drinks he liked sipping though she never said anything. Or maybe he was wrong, not as good at reading people as his mother had told him he was. As if he had a gift, she'd said. And maybe his mother was wrong when she insisted Susan was the sort to boss people around and cause a fuss if she didn't get her own way. So far she hadn't moaned about anything.

~

The man in the bottle shop gave Jeffrey a box for all the beers and a cooler bag for free for the wines, discount for six, see you tomorrow, wink, wink, ha-ha, very funny. At the dinner table, Jeffrey poured his wife a glass of wine, hoping to soften her pursed lips but she wouldn't touch it.

"If you don't, I will."

She shrugged and went and sat in the armchair where she picked up the tapestry she'd started when they were on honeymoon.

~

The longer Susan lived with Jeffrey, the more she realised drinking was a selfish man's game. Or woman's. Men and women should be equal. It annoyed her that he couldn't seem to enjoy life until the glaze hit his eyes. Not enjoy. Enjoy was the wrong word. Live. It annoyed her that he couldn't live an actual day, being able to converse, eat, read, unless he had alcohol in his hand. A giddy excitement overcame him when it was nearly his watering time and bam, after the first glass was poured he'd beam, all happy with the world and in the best of moods, except one drink wasn't enough. He had to keep going. And tipsy wasn't good enough, he had to be slaughtered. And it was like a slaughter, all the empties lying round the living room, cigarette ash on the coffee table that Susan had bartered so hard to get a bigger discount on, her first owned piece of furniture, sprays of beer on the walls where he'd opened the can too soon before sitting, all the fizz frothing to get out, spurting from the opening. Jeffrey didn't care where it ended up staining.

She thought of joining in sometimes like when they'd courted but the lack of memory of what she said and got up to when she was drunk didn't sit well. If a person wasn't in control of themselves, if they couldn't remember what they'd done in those blacked out hours, what was their history and who even were they?

~

"What's this?"

"Bread."

"Why's it brown?"

"Why do you think?"

"I don't like brown bread. I like white. Brown's disgusting."

"So go buy white."

"You do the shopping. You buy it."

"What?"

"You're the woman. You should buy me the bread I like."

"Why?"

"To make me happy."

"Bread's what makes you happy?"

"You know what I mean."

"No I don't. Explain it to me."

She kept hold of the knife she was using to spread the butter. He spoke to her like she was deaf or stupid.

"You're the wife. You do the shopping. Go buy me white bread for my toast, woman."

Susan had him up against the wall so fast he laughed thinking it was a joke but as she pushed the thumb of her left hand against his adam's apple and the knife in her right hand to his throat, Jeffrey cottoned on that it wasn't. Even though he knew the knife wasn't sharp enough to cut his skin, it was the anger, the gesture, the difficulty in breathing that got to him. Her eyes were full of hate, her breath pushed back his adding to the suffocation. Her knee pressed onto his thigh, hurting his leg as well as his head and shoulders.

"Dare to say that again and I won't be responsible for what I do to you." Her spit landed on his lips and he let it roll down his chin, unable to turn his head to the side so he didn't have to look at her. "Do you hear me? Do you hear this woman?" Jeffrey wished his mother was there. She'd get the mad lady off him. "Don't you ever. Ever. Speak to me like that again."

She let go of him, picked up her toast and sat down at the table. He did the same, eating quickly, heading to the bathroom, locking the door so she couldn't catch his shaking hands as they opened the hip flask. It clattered against his teeth as he necked a third of the contents straight down. He wasn't even that keen on whiskey, not any more, not since he'd discovered rum which looked a bit like blackcurrant juice which was easier to get away with at work, making the days more relaxing.

Susan

Susan had a set of keys for the drugs cupboard at the hospital, the rule being to always open it when another nurse was present, making sure no-one stole a bottle of pills for a relative or was tempted themselves to become addicted. It was impossible to swipe drugs from the cupboard but on the rounds, in public, it was easy because no-one expected such audacious stealing. The hospital administrators couldn't imagine anyone being so brazen and Susan was like a magician using slight of hand and distraction techniques to make her tricks successful.

"Good morning Agnes. How are you today?" Nurse Margaret asked while Susan picked up the patient's medicine cup from the trolley.

Agnes couldn't answer. She hadn't spoken since her stroke. She had no relatives as far as Susan could tell, none who cared, no-one who came to visit, none that would notice her dying.

"Here we go darling," Susan said, lifting the old lady's chin and prying open the patient's mouth. "Who's next?" she asked. When Margaret was checking the sheet, Susan slipped Agnes's three pills into her uniform's front pocket before holding the empty cup against Agnes's lips followed by the water. "There we go, all done. Well done dear."

"Mrs McMahon," said Margaret.

She was of no use to Susan, too on the ball.

And Mr Ringer, his wife was always by his side.

Mrs Maryland had four daughters who took it in turns to sit by her bed. Constantly. Why did they bother, raged Susan, she was asleep for most of the god-damn time.

Mr Jenkins. Perfect. Alone. Ready to die. Furious when he'd first regained consciousness and realised he'd been resuscitated.

"I saw a white light. I was quite happy to go. It was peaceful and there was no pain for the first time in eleven years. I saw the white light, was floating happily towards it. Why the hell did you have to go and save me?"

~

At home Susan opened her ladies day drawer that made Jeffrey squirm and added the day's haul to her collection. She knew roughly what each pill achieved at what dosage. She knew better than the doctors which medicines should be given to who, when and why, what would happen if too much was administered, or too little. So her mother was wrong. She could have been a doctor. She was clever enough and it wasn't fair that they said her being a girl and a bit strange meant she wasn't allowed to even try for it.

~

Mr Jenkins gripped her arm. Susan hated any physical contact when it wasn't her in control of it. She started to prise his fingers off her wrist bone.

"I've been watching you missy." Susan stopped still, letting his hand remain fixed on hers. "Can you swap mine for the sleeping ones, strong enough that I don't wake up again? I bet you know how to do that don't you sweetheart?"

She contemplated proclaiming her innocence but what was the point? Susan always hated it when people lied or denied when it was clear what the truth was. Sometimes black was black and white was white and people needed to face up to that rather than pretend that things were different. He squeezed her wrist harder, a mean hint to his eyes, still a bully as he approached his eightieth year.

"Well?"

"If you like."

"Good girl."

He let go of her hand, reached sideways and slapped her on the arse. She leant in closer, smiling.

"Do that again, dare to do that again and I'll make sure you go out in such agony you'll remember the pain even in the dead world, even in the hell that's expecting you, you nasty, dirty old bastard."

He pushed his head back into the pillow, eyes down at having met a match, in need of her help for his journey. She pulled the curtains around his cubicle, took his wallet from the side cabinet and handed it to him. He pulled out fifty dollars.

"That's all you've got?"

"I could write you a cheque."

"Like that won't look suspicious. Idiot."

"Then it's all I've got."

"It'll do I suppose. When do you want it?"

"Tonight?"

"I'm not on shift tonight. It'll have to be tomorrow."

Mr Jenkins felt the fear. What if the confession with the priest hadn't worked and God was watching, knew he was still a meanie, and as a punishment sent him to the bad place rather than up the stairs to have dinner on a cloud with his wife who was looking forward to him arriving, wasn't she?

"You'll be fine," said Susan. "It's me doing the deed so no blame will rest on your shoulders. If there is a purgatory, you won't be trapped in it. I'll take responsibility."

Susan stuck to her word as she always did. The end was quick and painless. Mr Jenkins found peace and Susan replaced the pills she'd brought in from home with her deceased patient's medication, happy with the exchange because the pink tablets were a particular favourite and he was a horror on the ward, none of the staff could stand him.

~

Jane stood in front of the door to Susan and Jeffrey's apartment, her right hand raised to knock but suddenly hesitant. On the other side of the door, Susan waited for the rat-a-tat-tat having heard a car door slam in a tone she recognised. After peaking out of the window her suspicion had been confirmed as she watched her mother-in-law balance something in her arms as she struggled to lock her car, it being important that she didn't drop whatever it was she was holding.

"I've brought some chocolate cake. Next time I think I'll bring a cheesecake. It's his favourite, was his favourite, still is I'm sure. He needs a dessert every night. It's good for his blood, for his blood sugar levels, otherwise he goes all wobbly. Lemon's always been his first choice since he was diddy. What flavour do you bake him?"

"I don't."

"What do you mean you don't?"

"Desserts rot the teeth and a set is meant to last a lifetime. Sugar ends up causing nothing but pain."

"I can show you how. It's very simple. Even you could manage it, I'm sure. I'll write out the recipe and—"

"I'm too busy to bake. I work longer hours than him you know."

"But you said you'd look after him."

"I am looking after him. And he could do with losing a few pounds, if he doesn't he'll have a heart attack. One of the doctors said as much when I introduced Jeffrey to him and he should know after studying for five years in medical school. As soon as he clocked Jeffrey's red cheeks at such a young age he told me he knew, he could tell, that Jeffrey needed to watch what he ate, being twenty years old and already boasting such a rosy pallor."

Jane placed the chocolate cake on the counter which she then placed her hands on, needing to keep hold of the support it offered. This wasn't what she'd imagined at all. Wasn't the new bride supposed to giggle and be grateful for catching a kind one who had prospects and two parents who owned their own home? She glared at Susan who was reluctantly putting the kettle on. She did not like her, not one bit.

"I just realised I've an appointment to get to. It completely slipped my mind, can you believe it? I'm afraid I haven't got time for a cup of tea. You have yours. I'm sure you're thirsty from working the long hours you're always telling me about. I'll see myself out."

Susan carried on making her drink. Once she'd heard the car door clunk, the engine start, a revving as Jane accelerated to her non-existent meeting, she picked up the cake and tipped it into the bin, covering the bits that showed with two paper bags from the greengrocers.

~

The next Saturday afternoon when Jeffrey was at the pub as he always was on a Saturday, Jane appeared with a lemon cheesecake which was the size of the large serving plate Susan and Jeffrey had been bought as a wedding present, which hadn't been unwrapped yet. Jane unwrapped, washed and cleared a shelf on their fridge for it, determined to still spoil her son.

When Jeffrey got home he was deliriously happy to see the treat. The first mouthful made him crave more sugar. He shovelled it into his gob in a way that made Susan balk and despise his pathetic need for sweet things. Wasn't there enough sugar in the booze he downed, his breath smelling of beer and cider that he belched across the room every evening. A pungent mist would hover below the ceiling meaning Susan had to air the apartment every morning.

When John arrived to collect Jane, he stayed standing up in the living room rather than take the seat Jeffrey offered. He watched Susan more than his son, smiling unsurely at her so she wondered did he realise their boy wasn't the easiest of souls to be partnered with in life. Was her father-in-law glad he'd got him married off so he was no longer his and Jane's problem, or no longer his problem, his wife seemingly unable to let go of her boy so he could get on with his new family. Not family, marriage, just a wife. The mention of family turned Susan's stomach.

"I can make you another one for next week darling. Would you prefer vanilla this time?"

"To be honest I love the lemon Momsi. You make the best lemon cheesecake in the state, the hemisphere."

"Oh my darling, darling boy. Of course. Lemon it is for my champion."

Jane kissed her son's cheek. He hugged her tightly and if he was a child Susan bet he would be whispering *please take me away from here I don't like it*, into his mother's ear as if she was leaving him at a boarding school full of cold corridors and horrid mean ones. *Take me with you, I'm begging you. I'll be as good as gold if you do, I promise. Tell daddy I'm coming home with you, no arguments, please Momsi.*

Was it a child she'd married? A boy in a man's body, wobbly belly protruding over the top of his trousers that he buttoned up below his waist. His inability to control what he ate and drank infuriated Susan. Inside. She didn't let it show, not yet. She merely pursed a lip to give him a clue that she disapproved.

He closed the door on his mother and turned to her with a leer.

"Fancy some you know what?"

She pushed him away.

"Keep your sweaty hands to yourself. You disgust me."

~

Susan heard Jeffrey lock the bathroom door. She stopped pinning her hair to listen, such good hearing she had, and sight, making up for the lack of taste. Metal. The sound of metal on metal meaning he was unscrewing the hip flask she'd found at the back of the towel cupboard, as if she wouldn't look there. Who did he think laid out their washing? It made her cross that she'd married someone so stupid. Champion indeed. His mother was delusional, same as hers had been but the other way round. Susan's mother had told her she would never be a champion, nor loved, nor liked nor wanted as she was less than mediocre which didn't bear well for her placing in the world. But her mother was wrong. Susan was clever. She'd got the top marks at nursing school the whole way through training. And she made things happen, things other people didn't dare to imagine.

Jeffrey flushed the chain to cover up his sneaking. A flask in the bathroom, two in the car, one in the front room on the floor, behind the sofa. Why did he hide them? To pretend to himself as well as her that it wasn't a problem? What others couldn't see couldn't hurt him? It must cost a lot though. Whiskey wasn't cheap or the nightly beers and expensive wines he ordered once he was half cut in a bar or restaurant. The receipt she'd found in his trouser pocket the previous Sunday showed he'd wasted nearly a day's wages on drinks while she was working a double shift to increase their savings.

That wasn't fair.

But at least it meant he was more malleable. She could get him to agree to just about anything when he was drunk. It was how he'd written the cheque and signed the lease in his name alone for their apartment while she squirreled away as much money as she could into her own separate bank account, the one she'd set up just for herself, for her future.

~

Susan pushed the armchair into the corner of the room, right against the two walls so no adult could fit in the triangular space behind it. She could have as a child, slipped under the chair and into the gap, holding her breath so her mother didn't find her. But now she was an adult in charge of her own life so instead she sat in the chair with her back right against it and pulled her feet onto the cushion, knees hugged into her chest so no-one could get to her. No baddie could grab her feet and pull her off, bump, bump, bump, making her bang her back and head on the floor.

She watched the empty room. She watched the door and its handle. She let her heart feel sad as nobody could see her and therefore take advantage of the weakness that was in her, buried deep down. She hadn't expected it to come out today and now it had reared its head she couldn't control it. Yet. She would in a moment.

She let herself wish she was like other people. They all seemed to have a spring in their step and smiles on their faces. If someone else smiled at them they'd smile back rather than glare furiously as they went to and from work. The other nurses joked around in the corridors, the toilets, the milk bars they visited on a day off, glammed up in their best dresses and lipstick.

Susan owned a lipstick, she fitted in that far. When she wore her Radiant Red, people stared at the dark hair contrasting with the pale skin, the bright lips and her legs that were so shapely. She knew they were, not just because Jeffrey had told her so. When people admired her she understood what they were looking at, how she stood out from others, but it gave her no pleasure. Which was fine. Except for now, today, when the maudlin feelings had taken over. She hugged her knees in even tighter.

How quickly time passed when you were thinking of nothing, much faster than a shift at work. Her limbs felt heavy like that time when she didn't have enough money for bus fair and had to walk eleven miles home, uphill and down. She couldn't be bothered to move, eat, drink. Staring at nothing was enough to keep her going, that was her sustenance. Until slowly, gradually a tingle made her wiggle her toes. She thought of all the things that annoyed the hell out of her, people walking slowly, people wasting food, people, so that by the time Jeffrey got home two hours later than he'd promised he would, demanding his dinner, she snapped, "It's in the bloody bin." He jumped at her shout then scuttled past her into the bathroom. She followed him, knocked gently on the door.

"Sorry to snap. A patient died today. It was upsetting. Can you come out? I need to show you something."

Susan poured the last of a bottle of red into a glass and put two A4 sheets on the table.

"I need you to sign those."

Jeffrey frowned. "Why?"

"I told you already. Stop being so silly pretending you don't remember. Here and here, and there plus on that line where there's an x next to it." She put the pen in his hand and placed the nib on the dotted line of the first document. "Your mother dropped round an apple pie. I'll put it in the oven as soon as you've finished. There's fresh cream to go on the side."

He signed where she'd pointed. So there was the life insurance, paid for and sorted. Sad bastard, Susan thought, not sympathetically but with a loathing, a sick feeling in her stomach that she'd have to put up with him until she'd made the right amount of use of him. When he walked into the wall, every evening he ended up walking into a wall on the way to the bathroom, she wished she could grab the back of his head and bash it against the plaster again and again and again until he was gone like Mr Jenkins.

Calton

Cal sat with his back against the wall that ran alongside the river. When he'd finished his ham sandwich, he closed his eyes and allowed the heat from the sun to soothe him. It was one of the best things in life as far as he was concerned, the sun sharing its warmth as it pressed on Cal's skin in a kindly way, pushing goodness through his pores, down his veins, happy thoughts into his brain, right to the core of it. The heat melted the tension the last six months had trapped inside him. A face pointed towards the sun was the best thing, the simplest and the best. The simplest things were often the best he was finding: a good meal after a hard day's work, a good sleep behind a closed door, teeth brushed in the morning, a chunk of chocolate sucked in the evening after a smoke.

He loved his smokes. A little weed went a long way in making him sleep well and feel as contented as he was exhausted after a day in the gardens. Which was what he needed too. Physical work that made him so tired he couldn't imagine staying up to drink beer after beer in the pub like the office boys did. Instead, he headed to the bottom of the garden next to his lodgings, just within the boundary of the Botanic Garden's land. There, five stone steps led to an overgrown patch of grass that no-one else seemed to visit or care for except Cal. He'd put a cushion inside a shallow cave that was curved into the stone. Once he'd stomped around and if it was dark, pointed his flashlight to check for scorpions and snakes, half-heartedly looking, not really caring if one bit him or not because there wasn't a future he was particularly desperate to hang onto, he'd sit back, spark up, enjoy the calm.

"Malcolm wants you at the Rose Garden."

A brown boot kicked the base of his black boot. He squinted up at Grant, confused at being torn out of his daydream.

"You'd better hurry. He's got a monk on. He's shouting that you were meant to be there twenty minutes ago."

Cal couldn't work out where the time kept running off to.

Susan

The envelope was addressed to Mr and Mrs J. Jeffreys. Inside it was a card from Jane and John, wishing Susan and Jeffrey a happy three month anniversary. Susan was sure she could sense the trauma her mother-in-law had experienced putting pen to paper, writing in a jolly tone as if the couple's future would be perfect and she cared deeply for both of them. The fact that she knew their address and could drive to the apartment, turn up whenever it suited her, infuriated Susan. It was Susan's life, her home, her private life, Jane should have no part of it and know nothing about it. How dare she drop round a card? Susan swept it onto the floor with the edge of a tea towel, not wanting her skin to touch the paper Jane's fingers had gripped, the paper her mother-in-law's skin had pressed down on, the ink that had flown from her pen. She wished the card was made of china so it smashed into hundreds of pieces but instead it lay there taunting her with its wholeness and lack of hurting. She kicked it but it just turned a couple of inches in the air and floated down to the ground again. She stamped on it, hard. Stamp. Stamp. Stamp. Stamp.

"Die you utter bastard of a card. Get out of my life. Don't dare tease me."

Stamp. Stamp. Stamp. Stamp. Kick. Kick. Stamp.

She did not want the card, didn't want it in her apartment, didn't want it near her reminding her that her parents-in-law existed when she never wanted to see them again. The point of marriage was meant to be freedom from parents. She'd go crazy if they arranged another visit. She'd pluck the skin from her fingers and scratch it off her legs, the haphazard cuts making it look like she'd walked through a patch of cacti.

As she twisted the card in her gloved hands in the same way she got water from a freshly washed towel, it occurred to Susan that her mind might be tainted. She knew that if a person was standing in front of her at that moment she'd hurt their body as well as their feelings as well as the card and she understood how people committed murder when a rage was upon them, not remembering any of it afterwards. She wouldn't be able to stop herself from crushing an arm, squeezing the bones on the hands, kicking the legs, punching the face, again and again and again, over and over where it didn't matter how much blood was gathering between her fingers. She'd keep going until her muscles hurt and she was so exhausted from the effort that all the rage could do was simmer beneath the surface as it was meant to in humans. She must be faulty, like a flickering electric light she needed to be fixed, tweaked so she worked like other people did.

"God-damn frigging bastard frigging cuntish fucking cunt fuckers," Susan muttered on repeat, knowing Jeffrey wasn't near. He must not see her having as big a rant or hear her cursing so crudely. That was not the Susan she knew, not quite, even though it was the real one, or half of her, maybe seventy per cent if she was being honest.

Did other people fly from nought to ten to capable of murder? She hadn't seen anyone else act like that apart from her dearly departed mother but perhaps that was because they hid it like Susan tried to. It was always in her, controlled until a trigger would make her want to bash the walls until the plaster crumbled, smash a car until the metal was dented, kick a door until her toes ached, fast kicks, bam bam bam bam, bastard wood on the bastard doorframe.

~

When Jeffrey arrived home the card was sitting on the side table in the dining area, warped and crinkled but just about standing upright. He picked up the phone, not asking about the twisted cover and frayed edges. His mother answered on the second ring. Susan escaped the apartment with the excuse of needing to buy milk so she could walk round the block counting her footsteps so as not to get wound up by their pointless chattering: one, two, three, four, five, six, seven, eight, eight, seven, six, five, four, three, two, one, one, two, three, four, five, six, seven, eight, eight, seven, six, five, four, three, two, one.

~

Jane rested her cup of tea on the table.

"Are you thinking of having children soon? I'd love to hear the pitter patter of tiny feet. We'd help out in any way we could, of course we would. Wouldn't it be marvellous? I'm so excited I can barely breathe. Jennifer, Margaret, Lauren and Louisa, they've all got grandchildren, nine between them and a tenth on the way. I can't wait to be a grandmother. They keep asking me when it will happen, made me promise I'd pass on their enthusiastic questioning to you. What shall I say? That you're trying and there should be good news any week now?"

Susan winced. My body. My body and if there's a baby, my baby, not yours. How could you think you'd have any right to a child that I went to the trouble of making and carrying? The assumptions the world made infuriated her. What was wrong with people? How dare they think they had a say in another person's life, another person's body. No-one did. They all thought they did but really, how dare they? God-damn church had a lot to answer for, all those men in robes telling people how they ought to act this way or that way, always their way, demanding that a person feel guilty for any different sort of feeling. The second best thing about leaving the home she grew up in was never having to go to church again, never having to kneel or pray or sing again. She'd never forgotten the smell of the incense or the priest's incendiary sermons and the time, that time, that week, that day, that trouble, the trouble she'd caused.

~

Susan and Alice had a rare conversation where for a moment they felt like sisters. They'd both agreed that neither of them liked going to mass. The priest was mean rather than nice. Would God really be glad that his messenger shouted at everyone every Sunday from the beautifully carved pulpit as spit fell from the sides of his mouth? The front row sat with handkerchiefs ready to wipe away any extraneous liquid that landed on their skin which had been thoroughly cleansed with a Sunday morning bath in preparation for their visit to the Lord's house.

The sisters agreed to stand together in front of their

mother to tell her times were changing and they, as modern ladies, no longer wanted to attend church each Sunday morning, like the Kay family. Their mother and father didn't make them go, him with the long hair and no need to work because of his wealthy parents.

"Pardon?" was all their mother said.

They waited for her to look up from her book but instead she turned a page and carried on reading.

"Mother?"

"I said pardon. Are you deaf Susan? Deaf as well as stupid?"

Alice nodded at Susan. They'd agreed that as she was the eldest she'd speak up for them both.

"The thing is, please, we don't want to go to church anymore if that would be alright please. The Kays don't have to go and they live in a big house so it can't be a bad thing not to attend. They're still very well respected in the community. I mean, their grandad's a doctor so he knows the most about everything."

Alice's lower lip wobbled as their mother read on and on. She started to step backwards out of the room but Susan grabbed her elbow and pulled her level with her. Mrs Brown looked up, put her book on the table by her side, switched the reading light off and rose from her chair, pushing down on non-existent creases on the skirt of her black dress.

"That's a definite *we* is it, as in the two of you standing together before me, half an opinion each, as in you've only one opinion between the two of you?" She loosened the navy scarf she always wore round her neck to protect it from drafts. "Alice. Is it possible you've been manipulated into standing beside your older sister today?"

Alice didn't know what manipulated meant. Was it the elbow grab because if it was then that's what Susan had done so that would be a positive right then yes Miss.

"Maybe."

"You may go. Chop chop. Don't dawdle."

Confused, Alice looked at Susan who'd changed from glaring at their mother to glaring at her little sister with furious, frightened eyes that made it clear she was planning on how she'd deal with Alice later.

"Actually, I—"

"Now. Immediately Alice. There's to be no nonsense or I shall get cross with you and we don't want that do we darling?"

Alice ran up the stairs to her bedroom. She hugged the teddy bear the granny in England had sent over, one to each of them, hers pink, Susan's brown.

Rather than being asked to repeat what she'd said or explain the meaning of her demands and questions, Susan was marched to the priest's house. Her mother's fingers pressed into the crook of her shoulder, right under the bone as if she was a cut of beef hanging in the butcher's refrigerated room, no blood dripping but the muscle torn and bruised where the hook had damaged the flesh. Standing outside the priest's house which stood next to the church, Susan wilted at the familiar feeling of dread in her stomach about the humiliation that was ahead of her. But the priest was out. So Susan was marched home, her mother even more furious because she'd wanted her child cursed and doomed, squeezed and pinched, poked hard by the priest, to accompany the spume of disappointment and despair she'd railed at her pathetic daughter. Susan zoned out in order to make it hurt her insides less, funny how words could hurt as much as thumps. Then she zoned in on how angry she was with her little sister whose fault it was that Susan alone was being punished. She would get her later, the god-damn bitch making their mother cover Susan in an array of teeny bruises.

~

Alice looked under the bed, under the sheets, in her wardrobe, in her dressing table drawers, in the living room, in the kitchen. She even snuck into her parent's bedroom though why on earth would it be there. She knocked on Susan's bedroom door.

"Have you seen my teddy?"

"No."

"Are you sure?" she called through the wood. "I can't find him anywhere."

"Yep."

"But I've looked everywhere and—" She jumped back, shocked at the door being opened.

"The Taylors were here this morning when you were out with daddy, the mother and her five boys. You know what they're like, unruly dirty blasphemers. I bet one of them took it."

"You think?"

"I saw the littlest one playing with it. Jackson is it, the curly haired toddler?" Alice felt like crying. How would she sleep without her teddy to hug, the only soft thing in her life? She needed him. "Tell mother. She'll be able to get it back for you."

Mrs Brown listened to her younger daughter tell of the youngest Taylor boy, with the curly hair, ringlets like a girl, playing with her teddy and now it was missing.

"You've looked everywhere?"

"Yes."

"You're sure?"

"Yes. I think so. Definitely."

"If I find out you haven't and it's in the house somewhere, you know the trouble you'll be in?"

"I couldn't have looked harder and where else would he be but in my bedroom? It's the only place I ever keep him."

Mrs Brown had not slept for the last three nights as she worried about her daughters' futures, neither of them seeming that bright nor pretty. Who would want to marry them and take them off her hands, though Susan had good legs, good cheekbones and they both had thick hair which she supposed was better than nothing. Thank God for small mercies etcetera etcetera, at least neither of them was a cripple like Melanie Harness's daughter. Yet now, in the middle of her exhaustion, a gift from England had been stolen from right under her nose by the very people she'd reluctantly invited in out of kindness, it being her turn according to Eleanor at the church of the Holy Trinity. Mrs Brown had not wanted those dirty, smelly people in her house. It had taken her hours to clean once they'd left, time and time again she had to wipe all their grubby hand prints off the windows, the mirrors, the bannisters, the door handles. And now something was missing, stolen, a prized possession that Alice had seen the two year old run off with. It made sense, though a decent mother would have returned the teddy once they'd found it in their child's arms, in their home or on the walk back there. Lucy Taylor obviously wasn't decent. The whole town knew she kissed men who weren't her husband while he was away mining in Coober Pedy, risking his life to make enough money to feed five children and his wife, who sometimes insisted on wearing the opals he found rather than letting him sell them. So they said. They said she said the blues and greens looked prettier on her than they ever would on a stranger. Such a selfish harlot, apparently.

Mrs Brown rode her bicycle across the railway tracks and banged on the unpainted wooden door. Lucy wiped her hands on her apron. Her hair was going prematurely grey. She wouldn't keep her looks or her husband for much longer, Mrs Brown reckoned.

"I believe you have Alice's teddy bear. A mistake I'm sure, Jackson didn't mean to steal it."

"Excuse me?"

"I believe you have Alice's teddy bear. I said it's a mistake I'm sure and Jackson didn't mean to steal it."

"I don't think so."

"May I check in the house?"

They stared at one another. Mrs Taylor did not want the lady with four bedrooms to see inside her one and a half roomed home.

"It's not here."

"Do you want me to call the police on your little boy? Do you want the whole town knowing about the thieves and miscreants you're raising?"

Mrs Taylor stepped to the side, ashamed of her house, her son, her life, the dirty plates on the table still covered in grease from that morning's bacon. She waited outside, not even bothering to try and hear the mumbles and denials or to comfort the crying toddler, not when that witch was in there. She'd do it later because at that moment, life was too heavy and she had no energy to rise and face it.

Mrs Brown stormed out, empty handed.

"He's hidden it somewhere. You better find it or I shall be wanting a replacement, forthwith and no excuses, chop chop, do you hear me? That was from Alice's grandmother, all the way from England. Can you imagine the cost of the postage alone?"

Lucy didn't understand some of the Queen lady's words which sounded angrier and louder as Mrs Brown rode her bicycle up the road. Before she turned the corner a sound came out of her like the animals made when they were fighting and fucking, screaming in the middle of the night.

"Jackson darling, come here for a cuddle. It's alright my love. The nasty lady's gone. Now tell mummy, did you get a new teddy?"

The toddler shook his head as he curled onto his mother's lap and into her shoulder. She hugged him tightly and kissed and kissed the top of his head.

"I didn't think so. Mummy loves you very much, you know that. She couldn't love you more. She thinks you're wonderful."

~

Alice knelt by her bed to say her prayers as her Mother watched to check she didn't skip any. When she opened her eyes she saw the edge of her teddy bear's paw sticking out from under her pillow, which wasn't possible, because she'd checked there, over, in and under the covers. It couldn't be right that she'd missed it.

"Hurry up and get into bed. Your knees will scar otherwise then who'll want to court you?"

"Look," Alice said, rather than trying to get away with her slack searching by finding the teddy in the garden, behind the bushes, down the road where she could have said Jackson must have dropped it. "I don't understand. I checked under there, I really did." She pulled her teddy from under the pillow and held it up to show her mother before hugging it. "I looked so carefully, everywhere. Naughty teddy. How did you get back there? Do you think the house is haunted? If not, how did Jackson put teddy back because Susan definitely saw him take it, she told me. I don't understand what happened," Alice wailed.

Mrs Brown pulled her child up from the floor by the elbow and squeezed either side of the bone. Alice's knees buckled.

"I went to their house. I accused her son of stealing it."

"I know," cried Alice. "I'm sorry. I'll go and tell them it was me, that I didn't look properly, that we know it wasn't them and we're sorry, that teddy's home so everything's alright now. They'll forgive us won't they?"

Mrs Brown spotted movement to her right. She quickly turned her head. Susan scarpered down the hallway and dived into her room. When her mother reached the side of her bed, she pretended to be asleep but her eyes were closed too tightly for it to appear realistic.

"It was you wasn't it? Punishing your sister for not going along with your getting out of mass plan." She pulled back the covers. Susan's bare legs erupted in goose bumps. It was cold in winter with no heating, unlike when they'd lived on the East coast. She preferred it there. "Get down on the floor." Susan did as she was told. "You're to lie there all night. No covers, no pillow. And I'll be watching. Dare to move and I'll hurt you. The shame you've caused me you little witch. Do you have any idea how much I hate you right now? I should send you back to

England to your granny, see how you like that, where's it's all so cold, dark, wet and windy and the company, she's always bloody miserable. You'd suit each other."

Susan slept fitfully, waking to see her mother staring down at her from under the covers of Susan's cosy bed. Her cheek hurt where the bone pressed against the floorboard. No position was comfortable. A chill settled in her bones, a cough on her lungs which turned into a bout of pneumonia. There was no money for medicines but the nurse who lived next door helped her through it. She told Susan the body's healing power was sometimes as strong as medicine and she could tell Susan was a fighter, meant to live a long life, not die yet, God love her the poor thing, it was so unfortunate she'd caught this rotten influenza. Spurred on by her first taste of kindness, Susan fought hard. She broke free of the fever and shallow breathing knowing that she wanted a future, her own future that she was in charge of, no-one else, definitely not a mother or husband or useless, silent man for a father. And the anger she felt towards them all, it proved to be a more powerful nourisher than caring. Anger would be her saviour.

~

Alice didn't visit Susan's room when she was ill. Instead, she tossed and turned, positive that she'd physically shrunk under the weight of the guilt that pressed down on her shoulders, the torment of not having stood beside Susan when they did the mass thing, at not having known what manipulation meant. She curled into the corner of her bed when she heard her sister up and about, footsteps approaching her bedroom.

Alice knew it would hurt, whichever bit Susan decided to grip, but it would be momentary and it was fair enough. She deserved it so she would take it. Susan walked to the foot of the bed. All she did was stare, and stare and stare. Alice went from looking into her sister's eyes to bowing down to peeking up to begging Susan to punish her. All Susan did was stare until Alice wept, full of shame and despair. Susan left without saying a word, quietly shutting the door behind her.

Susan

Susan couldn't get to sleep as she knew Jeffrey would be back from the pub any minute, waking her up with his teeth brushing, toilet pissing, snack making, unable to understand that as his wife had to get up in seven hours to complete a twelve hour shift she didn't want to talk to him or be bothered by his monstrous ablutions.

He asked her to go out with him some nights, to the pub or for a meal like when they first met but she always refused. That had been her ploy to catch him. It was not her. She didn't like those places or his company and now that she didn't drink it made her realise how boring a drunk was, how annoying they were to anyone who was sober.

Susan had treated men and women like him. Their liver malfunction turned their skin a tinge of yellow. The haemorrhaging from their throat or stomach was such an unpleasant way to die. A gruesome bloodied mess coated the walls and floors, took hours for the porters and cleaners to get rid of. There was a gurgling noise as the patient drowned in their own blood which took minutes, too many minutes, not a quick death compared to a knock on the head say or a heart giving out on a body.

Jeffrey's drinking was getting heavier.

She was sure of that.

There was the smell of him, the sweat he woke in each morning, pyjamas wet, sheets stained yellow, his skin steeped so deeply in alcohol that he could have bottled his perspiration and drunk it. There was the dullness of his chat, the embarrassment, the bravado, the loudness when he droned on and on as if what he had to say was more important than anyone else. The putting her down in the queue at the supermarket that one time, using her as an excuse for a joke, wanting a laugh at her expense except no-one laughed because he wasn't funny. She would not be talked to like that, not again, not in front of other people. She would not. He was a drunken bugger and she deserved better.

~

John and Jane arrived at five o'clock but their son didn't turn up so the three of them sat in silence, watching the clock, smelling the edges of the dinner burn. They finally moved to the table when Susan declared, "I'm serving now. If he's not here that's his problem."

"I'm sure it's a one off," Jane said. "Maybe he got the date wrong. Or he's working late, I bet that's it."

"On a Saturday?"

"I'll go and get him," offered John. "Which pub will he be at?"

"How should I know?" said Susan. "All I do is stay at home to cook and clean and go to work to earn us money, trying so hard to be a good wife. Sorry. Sorry, I don't mean to moan." She pretended to nearly cry, held her forehead in her fingers, took a deep breath and looked up with a smile. "Never mind. It's just such a shame that tonight of all nights he's gone missing, yet again actually, what with you two coming here rather than going to your bridge night and me spending all of my afternoon away from the wards cooking lasagne. It's your recipe Jane, his favourite though not as tasty as when you make it I'm sure."

Susan's voice caught in her throat just like she'd practised.

~

Jeffrey arrived home after his parents had left, nine thirty being nearly their bed time.

"But you said I should stay out as long as I liked today because you had a migraine and needed the peace," he protested.

"No."

"You did," he slurred, over-emotional from nine hours of boozing.

"No. You're wrong. I never said that."

Jeffrey was near to crying. He feared he was going mad, his brain no longer functioning. "I swear you did." He pictured that morning, him at the door, Susan giving him permission to be out until whenever. "I didn't know they were coming."

"You're drunk," she said. "That's why you can't remember."

"But I would have come back. Lasagne's my favourite."

"You'd better call them to apologise, tell them what happened."

"But you didn't tell me they were coming."

"Yes I did. You need to stop saying that. You are wrong and I am right and your parents said I'm a saint for putting

144

up with you. Christ almighty, they don't even know the half of it."

~

Jeffrey stood in front of his wife, sheepish, mortified. She didn't look up. He waited for an acknowledgement. Waited longer. She carried on with her sewing, eyes down, focused on her tapestry. He twisted his hands together. Such a child, she thought, seeing the movement in her periphery vision, so frigging foolish.

"What have you done?"

"Is it tomorrow the rent's due?"

She rested her sewing onto her lap.

"You know it is."

"The thing is…"

He curled his toes inwards. Susan could not bear his clichéd behaviour.

"Out with it."

"I lost my pay."

"How?"

He shrugged his shoulders and scratched the new cut sitting on top of an egg bruise on his head, peeling off half the fresh scab, giving a dribble of blood the freedom to run down his forehead.

"Maybe you got robbed but were so drunk you don't remember."

"That could be it." He jumped on her theory. "Yeah. You know when I came round I had this bump and cut on my head. They must have knocked me out. That's it. Some bloody bastards robbed me."

"Poor Jeffrey. That must have been so frightening."

"I wasn't scared, just outnumbered."

"Of course. Poor, brave Jeffrey." She got him a beer. "You deserve this."

Thrilled. He was thrilled. This was going a thousand times better than he'd expected.

"Thanks doll."

She scowled at the back of his head. Not your doll. Not your toy, never your plaything.

"So the rent, you've got none of it?"

"I can't believe they got me on pay day. Maybe they followed me. I bet that was it. They'll have known the day we all got paid and waited until I was on my own to grab me. Bastards the lot of them. I think there were three but there may have been four; there was no way I could have beaten them." He glugged down his drink. "I don't suppose you've any money?"

She knew that he knew she did. Of course he did. That's why he had the confidence to spend all of his, because he knew there was a backup and when it came to money, she wouldn't fail them.

"I do. As it's not your fault and an emergency." After his third beer she added. "There's one condition though Jeffrey, to me paying the rent rather than you calling your parents for the money like last month. We need to think about moving. I mean look at what happened to you, an innocent, hard-working man attacked on your way home and it could have been a lot worse so thank the Lord it wasn't but I won't rest easy now when you're out in the day or the night time. Something about this place isn't right. We've never been happy here have we? And now that you've been beaten it feels like fate that I've found us somewhere better to live."

He laughed. She'd lost him with her ramblings. He was

finding it hard enough to stay sitting upright without having to listen and think too.

"You won't lose the rent again will you?"

"No way."

"Promise?" He nodded solemnly. "And we'll move. You're alright with that."

"I dunno."

"Do you want to get hurt again? Robbed? Murdered? Is that it?"

"No."

She took his empty glass and filled it to the brim.

"All I'm trying to do is look after you Jeffrey, like your mother asked me to. You know she's worried you drink too much? I said it was that you didn't eat enough, nothing to do with the amount of alcohol in your system but maybe she's right, I mean—"

"You're the one who's right."

"I am aren't I? I agree. I think so too." She passed him a cigarette and held up the lighter. "You can't go back on your word, not now you've promised. You did mean it when you agreed didn't you? Tell me I haven't married a liar."

He rested his head on the back of the sofa. Tired. Confused. He tried to remember the conversation but there were too many blanks where he should have been listening to her and had instead drifted off into thinking about cheesecake.

"I'd never lie to you, I promise. Is there still some of Momsi's dessert in the fridge?"

Calton

Cal settled himself at the back of the gardens. He sat cross legged and lit his spliff, letting go of the day, work done with until tomorrow. The sky was clear, the stars sharp, his muscles tired. He closed his eyes as he smoked.

Five tokes in, a woman's squeal startled him so much he jolted his neck, banging the back of his head on the rock, feeling a crush and shot of pain jettison through his right shoulder. He pulled hard on his smoke then moved his arm back and forth in front of him, trying to loosen the spasm.

"Where is it? I can't see anything."

"Just up there. Come on you gorgeous thing you," a man replied.

Cal knew that voice from somewhere. The woman shrieked as if in fear but to Cal it sounded like she was putting it on for attention. The darkness rustled in front of him. Cal shuffled back on his bum like a baby not yet ready to crawl until he reached the back of the cave which was only three foot from the entrance. They'd better not be heading his way. The trouble he'd be in. Staff weren't meant to be in the gardens after dark. That was one of the rules that really couldn't be broken. Four feet stopped to his left, he could reach out and grab their calves, scare the life out of them. He nearly giggled at the thought, a part of him tempted.

"What's that smell?"

"What?"

"I can smell something weird, like burning."

"That's your loins on fire for me doll. Now come here would you."

A waist was hooked into a flabby stomach. Cal reckoned he'd be alright. They were caught up in each other, a temporary stop before moving to their love lair no doubt. He sucked in hard. The end of his smoke glowed like a firefly, four seconds in, two seconds holding it in his mouth, three seconds out.

"There it is again. Can't you smell it?" Feet and legs parted. The lady's legs turned full circle. "Where's it coming from? There's something on fire, I tell you."

"Forget it would you. We—"

"I've got a great sense of smell, same as my Aunt Lydia. Sometimes I even smell things in my dreams and when I wake it's the same smell that's coming up from downstairs so it's kind of like I'm psychic." She bent down, poked her head into the cave and screamed. "There's someone in there." She stumbled backwards.

"What? Don't be stupid woman."

A man's body bent down and his face poked in front of Cal's like a Moray eel from a gap in the rocks, deep under the water. It was the Marcus White, Head of the Greenhouses. And the woman next to him wasn't the wife he'd agreed to grow old with for richer for poorer.

"Who's there?" His voice trembled. Cal quickly rubbed the spliff's butt into the floor and covered it with dirt as best he could. In the dark they shouldn't be able to find it. "Come out. Now. Or I'll call the police on you, you little shit. Don't think I don't mean it."

Cal crawled forwards. The man stepped back, giving him room to stand. The woman curled behind Marcus who was trying to act like he had all the authority.

"What were you doing in there?"

"Nothing."

"He was smoking drugs," the woman said. "Like the hippies down by the bay. That's where I've smelt it before. The bunch of chancers."

"Is that right? Were you smoking drugs son?"

The hesitation made Cal's denial sound pathetic. "No."

"He was. He was Marcus. That's against the law. You should call the police."

"Don't you work in Tom's team? Carlton is it?"

"Calton."

"Not any more. You leave in the morning."

It crossed Cal's mind that he could blackmail Marcus into letting him stay but what use would that be if he couldn't have a smoke and chill out by himself each evening. Or he could tell on them. But what was the point of Cal having it on his conscience that he'd ruined two marriages and hurt the feelings of the cheaters spouses when given time they'd find out for themselves, they were bound to.

"Will I get paid until the end of the month?"

"No," the man laughed. Cheek of the little bugger.

"Wouldn't your wife want me to?"

"You little shit, I—"

The woman put her hand on her lover's arm.

"What's ten days wages? Then he'll be gone and everyone's a winner. That's right isn't it Calton?"

"Yes Ma'am. Absolutely."

Susan

Susan stood next to Fran in the canteen.

"I saw you."

"Pardon?"

"And after I saw you sneak them into your shoe, the red pills, did you sell them or swallow them with your friends or are they tucked into the bottom of a sock in the back of a drawer purely for emergencies? Are they for when your head feels like there's a clamp squeezing your skull until you're sure it's about to pop, pop, pop, like an abscess you've pricked on a patient, all the puss oozing out, satisfying, cleansing. Is that why you take them?" The fear on her colleague's face delighted her. "Perhaps on a night out you mix them with the gin I've heard you're so fond of? I personally haven't smelt it on your breath so don't you worry about that though Deborah has, and Margaret, Jane, Patricia. They were discussing whether or not to mention it to the Sister and I wondered, is that what you do to escape your unhappiness? Pop a couple of red pills with a large G and T or perhaps a glass of chilled white wine, a really big one. Does that make it easier to forget the past or is it the present you're hating?"

"No," said Fran as she clutched her tray, close to tears. "I would never do that. You can't drink on them."

"Why not?"

"That'd make you go doo-lally. You should never have alcohol with the red ones."

"Fancy that. I never knew. Me a nurse and all. So there we go then Fran, onwards and upwards, doing the best we can in this life that can be such a trial, don't you think? Why aren't you answering me? What do you think Franny Fran Fran?" Susan leant in closer. Her breath coated Fran's cheek, squeezed between the gaps in her teeth. "At least you're not one of those aggressive ones who blames the world and shouts at others because of how you're feeling. Or are you? Is it simply that I haven't seen that side of you?" Susan raised her voice. "God-damn it, the queue's slow today. Do you know what? I think I've lost my appetite. I have. I'm not hungry anymore. Ha!" Fran jumped at the loud, false laugh. Susan put her tray back on the help yourself pile. "I'll leave you in peace my darling and don't worry." She winked at the fearful girl. "I'll try my very best not to tell anyone about what you get up to. See you later Frances."

~

When Jeffrey leant over to put his socks on a fart escaped, its foul odour hitting Susan smack in the nose. She wasn't quick enough to dodge it. She wished it was her sense of smell rather than taste that she'd lost with the whack from her mother. At least then there would have been a benefit, perhaps she wouldn't mind him so much if she couldn't smell him. Had ever a man produced such rotten scents? Yeasty and thick as if there was a substance in the air rather than just an odour. She retched. The beer. Too much bastard beer in his system, the bubbles in the drink needing something to escape through. She was sure it was the beer he drank each night that made it so noxious as once when he'd had a cold he'd only drunk three bottles that evening and the amount of gas he produced the next day had definitely lessened. She held her breath and left the room. When she got back from work, she'd have to open the windows, staying in the room to make sure no poisonous spiders jumped in wanting to bite her, then close them again before bedtime.

~

Susan was put on drug duty with Felicity who she'd never seen not smiling apart from the one time she sat crying in the staff room because her Granny had died. Susan hadn't comforted her with there there's or hugged her like the other nurses did. She'd never met her own grandparents so didn't understand the bond they were all sympathising with and saw no point in trying to comfort a colleague with false platitudes.

"Mind if I push?" Susan asked. "I've got a heavy monthly, need to lean if you know what I mean."

"Sure thing," said Felicity. "I'd rather be handing them out anyway."

They filled the tubs with drugs then set off down the corridor. Susan pretended her stomach ached and leant further over the chest high trolley, making sure the containers were out of sight of Felicity, swapping a white aspirin that she'd coloured in red for one of the two red pills in each container. One right, one wrong. And it proved her theory correct that half the drugs they administered were useless as when she swapped the real ones for her placebos no-one ever noticed a patient not responding as the doctor had hoped they would, not when she changed over yellow, orange, pink, blue and now, it would be the same with the red ones. Susan believed diagnosis and prognosis were half guess work, half fact, the doctors saying it was this disease until it was proven it couldn't be this one so it might be that one, and so on and so on until the patient either died or was cured. Neither result was necessarily predictable even if afterwards the doctors all acted like that was what they'd expected to happen. Bloody doctors lording it over the nurses as if they knew so much more than them when their instinct was so lacking in comparison. She should slip a pill into a doctor's cup of tea, see how they liked it.

By the time the ninth round of the month's shift was finished Susan had added twenty one red, thirteen orange, five blue and three pink tablets to her collection. She only liked odd numbers. They were reassuring, helped her not get caught, she was sure of it. Even numbers made her feel like something bad was going to happen.

~

After the Radiant Red lipstick had been blotted and coated on her lips a second time, Susan stood beside the dining room table.

"I'm coming out with you tonight. Fetch my coat, there's a chill in the air. When I was coming home from work I could feel it."

As Jeffrey lifted his wife's coat off the peg, he wished she wasn't joining him. He'd only asked her to occasionally accompany him because she always said no. He didn't want her seeing how much money he spent on a night out, didn't want her meeting his drinking buddies. The pub was his world. She was not welcome.

"Here you go darling."

She pointed to the table where a red pill was sitting next to a glass of water.

"Don't forget your vitamin. I've had mine already."

As she fixed a red scarf around her neck, Susan watched Jeffrey in the mirror to make sure he swallowed his tablet. He held his arm out to her, determined that they appeared like a normal couple, telling himself not to be afraid of where they were going because when you looked at the facts she was a good wife who worked hard and cared well for him. The niggles he had about her sharpness, maybe he over imagined how she sounded because look at her cooking him such nutritious meals and never forgetting his vitamins. You'd only do that if you really loved someone.

~

The pub was so full of smoke Susan may as well have been sucking on the poisonous sticks herself. She was sure they were bad for a person's health. The patients with the green and brown phlegm spewing coughs admitted time after time with pneumonia, bronchial infections, hearts skewed in their workings, they were always the smokers.

They found a table in a corner and Jeffrey bought them both a beer. She raised her glass and, over-excited at his wife's niceness, keen to keep her happy, Jeffrey raised his and clinked it against Susan's but too hard so the liquid spilt over their fingers.

"Damn it. So clumsy. I'm sorry."

He grabbed a bar mat and tried to wipe the liquid off her.

"Don't touch me." When he paused with his arm mid-air, her tone softened. "It was an accident. Don't worry about it." She raised her glass again and smiled. "Cheers darling."

So unlike her normal self. Jeffrey decided this would be one of their best nights ever. He might even get to do the business with her.

~

The rattling of his teeth woke him up. He rolled onto his side but there wasn't a pillow to fluff air into or an eider-down to pull up and wrap around himself to get warm. There was a putrid smell in the air, too much beer last night, his guts in turmoil. Susan would be furious. Jeffrey reached below his knees for the cover that he must have kicked down the bed but couldn't get hold of it. He bent his elbow so his hand went behind his back, thinking it must have slipped over the edge of the bed in the night but instead of a soft sheet, his hand reached out onto a cold hard surface, an edge, the air, the hard surface again, no give in it like their mattress. He opened his eyes. Rather than a white wall, he was facing bricks painted green, no wallpaper, no wooden wardrobe, no dressing table. Rolling onto his back made his shoulders crunch. He groaned at the pain in his bones and using his right hand to balance, pushed himself to sitting too fast so he burped and was a bit sick in his mouth. He closed his eyes, managed to swallow it. Shouts echoed outside the door. He sat with his legs over the side of the bench. The floor was cold, grey stone rather than a dark red carpet. The noise of the metal slot opening made his teeth hurt. His head throbbed like a bastard.

"Jeffreys. You're going home."

The door was pulled open, its metal base scraping over the concrete floor. Jeffrey covered his ears to try and lessen the headache but was pulled up by his elbows and marched by a man in a navy uniform through gates and down corridors to a wooden door that opened into the lobby of the police station. Susan was signing a white piece of paper, two pieces of navy carbon paper between it and further yellow layers. When she looked up, he saw a bruise on her cheek. It crept under her left eye. He tried to remember the night before but all he could see was her and him in the corner of the pub, drinking, smiling, drinking. Three other ladies were sitting on a bench to his left, handbags on their laps. One looked sad, the other two were glaring at him, their lips pursed together so tightly it was as if their creator had forgotten to add a gap big enough for teeth to smile through.

Susan walked ahead of him out of the front doors. He scurried after her, the sunshine making him step backwards rather than forwards as he got used to the brightness. He stumbled on with his eyes half closed. His head hurt as if he'd knocked it with such force that the inside was bruised. His lungs were sore from too many cigarettes.

She did not speak on the walk home. Once they were inside the apartment Susan went into the bedroom and closed the door before he could follow, not that he wanted to considering the fury that was radiating from her. He lay on the sofa and fell asleep, was woken up by a kick on his arm.

"That's it? You're not going to apologise?"

"Sorry."

"For what?"

He looked at her cheek but couldn't believe it was him

who'd caused that damage because he'd never punched anyone in his life, not ever. He didn't understand how a person could hit another, hurt their skin, their bones, their organs on purpose, not even boy on boy let alone a man on a woman.

"Ending up in jail." She raised her foot as if to kick him on the leg. When he flinched, she lowered it.

"What happened?" he asked.

"You don't remember?"

He shook his head.

"Since when?"

"The pub."

"When in the pub?"

"Us sitting at the table. I think I'd got the third round in."

Utterly ashamed, he wasn't sure if he wanted to hear the sordid details.

"You got so drunk the barman had to help me carry you out of there. The weight of you leaning on me was too much for a woman to bear and when we were half way home I begged you to carry yourself. You started to get angry, screamed at me like a loon. A policeman heard the shouting, saw that a kerfuffle was about to become worse and offered to take you away. When I said yes please officer because my arms were hurting where you'd been pressing and I was desperate, desperate I tell you, you swung a punch at my lack of support, cracking me here. See the bruise Jeffrey. See what you did to me. The policeman insisted no arguments he's coming with us Ma'am, you come by in the morning, if – you – want – to – you – don't – have – to. No pressure. You can leave him to fester in the corner should you wish to Ma'am. But I'm soft. That's what the man at the desk said when I came to sign you out and now I'm not sure I should have done, not when you can't even find it in yourself to apologise."

Jeffrey tried to remember.

"I could have left you to rot. Or called your dearest Momsi and Popsi, asked them to pay the night's fee instead of me having to dip into my savings." He winced. His parents mustn't know what he was turning into. "Pah. I didn't think you'd like that. I won't tell them. If we move like you agreed, to a town away from that pub and those people who sit there all night rather than going home because they hate their lives within their houses. The deal is we move. I've arranged it all. We'll start again with you doing as I say instead of being known as one of those mean drunks people think so little of, a wife beater. Is that what you want people to whisper about you because that's what those who see my face will think and I won't correct them. Why should I?"

Jeffrey chewed on a nail rather than answer her, wishing the night hadn't turned into a blackout.

"Alright."

"And?"

"I'm sorry. I don't know how that happened. I can't remember any of it."

His voice caught like he was going to cry like a little boy found stealing a cookie, scared to burn in hell like his mother had told him happened to thieves and miscreants. Jeffrey rolled over to face the inside of the sofa. Marriage wasn't what he'd thought it would be. Tears ran down his cheeks. His wife mustn't see them. And his Momsi, she'd been right. She said it would end in tears, mark my words and no mistaking, and look at him curled up in the corner of the sofa, weeping like a baby.

Susan

The coffee table fitted into the back of the car, upside down. They put boxes of food between its legs, a box of saucepans to the side, their two suitcases on the backseat.

"You drive, I'll navigate," said Susan.

She directed him to the highway and the car was speeding along it before there was a chance to pull over.

"The country? Are we out in the sticks now?"

After an hour Jeffrey pulled into a petrol station.

"What's going on? Where are we going?" he asked.

"It's about another hour and a half, if that. Not far considering the vastness of this country."

Far enough away that the parents-in-law couldn't pop round but not so many thousands of miles across numerous states that she could be accused of stealing him.

"What about my job? I can't travel that distance each day."

"I resigned for you, after calling ahead to the municipal buildings who happened to be looking for a new administrator. It's at a lower level than your old job but you'll soon rise through the ranks what with the talent your Momsi is always going on about. The cost of the apartment is half of what our old place was, cheap enough to buy in fact, and there are two pubs on the high street, both less than a five minute walk from it. I don't mind if you spend time there, if you're feeling homesick and need to drown your sorrows. There'll be no nagging from me, no need to rush back for an unexpected visit from your parents."

She was prepared for anger, ready to fight back hard but without saying anything, Jeffrey got out of the car and lit a cigarette. She waited in her seat for him to return. He went into the petrol station and came back with a large bag of potato chips and two bottles of cola.

"I didn't like that job much."

"I know."

"Momsi will be heartbroken."

"You can visit them once we're settled. Write them a letter tomorrow and I'll post it for you."

"It doesn't feel right that we didn't say goodbye, had a party maybe and—"

"It's a new start for us." She put her hand on his thigh and undid his zipper. "I know I've been fractious since we got back from honeymoon, acting a bit peculiar. I'm sorry about that. It's not been fair on you and I've been thinking about it, how to work on being a better wife. I reckon that living so close to your parents, wonderful as they are, see-ing them so much, it reminded me of mine being dead and all that I was missing and have missed for so many years. Watching all that happiness and love made all this badness come out of me, an anger that I took out on you, my husband, making your life miserable when it should be joyous because you're one of the good ones." Her cold fingers made him shudder. "So us moving. That means I'll be a better wife, able to look after you properly, have dinner on the table when you're back from the pub, white bread if you want it. I mean what was I even thinking, who cares what type of bread you eat? There we go then." She pulled her hand back, flicked the gunk from it out of the open window and wiped the remainder off her fingers with a tissue from her bag. "We'd best get going. I said I'd pick up the keys by four thirty."

~

Their new apartment was white and bright, the carpet pale green, recently fitted, plain, no patterns in the whole place, which she'd insisted on. It was just like the real estate agent had described it on the phone. Good. Susan was glad he hadn't turned out to be an exaggerator and that no argument was needed there. As they were on the top floor of the block of six apartments, Susan opened a window with no fear that a burglar would sneak in though she never left them open at night as you never knew what might be flying through the sky, nasty, evil spirits waiting to enter an open mouth and possess a human being.

The hospital was a ten minute bus ride away at the edge of town. Jeffrey's job was a fifteen minute walk from their front door. The hospital buildings, morgue and local high school came under the care of the council and that was where she'd found her husband's entry level opening.

The neighbourhood was peaceful. You heard birds more than voices and it was friendly. People smiled when they passed each other on the street so Susan kept her head bowed rather than getting involved with the chats in the shops or the communal areas of their block. The hospital was much less busy than her old one. She read a book on her breaks and the other staff soon learnt to leave her be, thinking her personality was studious, tee-total, a little cold but so efficient that they all wanted to be on the same shift as her because she volunteered for all the jobs, even the dirty ones, preferring to be busy.

The town had a river that ran alongside it, into and out of it, steep banks on either side. Bendy roads meant you had to slow down at each loop-di-loop or you'd end up at the bottom of the water and wouldn't be the first to have drowned because of the speed which meant you'd over-run the corner. The river was deep. And it was dirty. A body could disappear under the surface and if there were no witnesses, never be discovered.

~

Jeffrey took up fishing with a man from his work called Roger who told him they could sink a few beers while they were hard at it, hard at it doing nothing. They both laughed at that one.

"The great outdoors," Jeffrey told his mother on the phone. "I love it. All the fresh air. And Roger's a great bloke, wait till you meet him. You'll think he's hilarious. You'll get on like a house on fire, I betcha."

"When can we visit darling? We'd love to see where you're living. It sounds so beautiful."

"Soon," he said. "Susan wants the apartment to be perfect first. Once the spare room's been decorated, that'll be your room and then you can visit as often as you like. I can't wait for you to see it."

It was easier calling his mother from work. At home he'd started to feel like he needed to watch what he was saying which was silly because Susan had said she didn't mind him speaking with his parents, but for some reason he couldn't shake the uncomfortable feeling that she wasn't being truthful.

~

Susan made sure the fridge was always stocked up with beer and encouraged Jeffrey to go out after work with his new friend. She found life easier when he was so drunk he forgot kissing existed. She'd rather that than him in bed wanting to do it which wasn't what she was on earth for, there had to be more to her existence. She did let him have sex with her occasionally, gave in sometimes, good boy and all that. Seven thrusts and he was done. She'd go to the bathroom and wipe the goo off her legs. When she got back into bed she'd back away from him and he'd sink sadly down to the edge of the mattress so anyone would feel sorry for him. Except maybe not once they saw the inside of his brain which was cluck, cluck, clucking for a drink rather than a cuddle with his Mrs.

~

Susan rested the back of her head against the bus seat, closed her eyes and swallowed hard, willing away the nausea. She'd felt fine at work, tired but not sick. She opened the window to the left of her seat but sweat still dripped from her hairline to jaw. Her stomach turned as her skin paled. Some god-damn bug from some god-damn dirty patient no doubt. When a burp rose, acidic bile at its base, she hurried off the bus five stops early and held onto a lamppost as she breathed out through her mouth, in through her nose. Fresh air was better than bus air, the warm breeze welcome. She closed her eyes for a second then took twelve steps across the road to the wooden bench that sat in front of the bottle shop. Her arms and legs twitched as if there were little electric currents running through them. She wished she could lie down as sweat dribbled down her back.

"Ma'am. Ma'am are you alright?" A bearded man was watching her, an unlit cigarette in one hand, bottle of booze in the other. "Would you like me to get you some help?"

"No."

"Are you sure? You don't look so good."

"Better than you smell," she mumbled.

"Excuse me?"

"Nothing."

Susan shooed him away with her left hand but when he budged it was to sit beside her. The smoke from his cigarette made her heave. She used the arm of the bench to push herself to standing and focused on getting from one block to the next, down the road, up the hill, across the park, through the apartment door, up the stairs and onto the sofa. She lay down, cheeks paler than the walls, head too heavy for her body, throat feeling as if it was swollen with the nausea it was trying to force down. Puke erupted into her mouth which she kept closed and covered with both hands as she ran to the toilet.

~

Jeffrey arrived home to a locked bathroom door. He banged on it, burping and farting at the same time, a burning pain in his bladder, desperate for a piss.

"Are you nearly finished? Let me in would you."

"I'm busy. You'll have to wait."

When Susan came out he was sluicing out the kitchen sink. She spotted eight splashes of orange urine on the work surface.

"Did you just piss in the sink?"

"No."

"Don't lie to me."

"I was desperate."

"You pissed in the kitchen sink?"

"No."

"Where I prepare the food?"

"I didn't. I was washing my hands, trying to get rid of the smell of the fish."

"What fish? There's no fish."

"Roger's. He caught some. I didn't."

Jeffrey backed into the fridge when she stepped forward.

"Is this what our life's going to be like? You spending all your time drinking while I'm left at home to cook and clean, wiping your vile piss stains off the kitchen worktop?"

"Oh shush," Jeffrey slurred, tired of her negativity. "That's what you're meant to do, what women are made for. You're not as clever as us men you know, or as strong."

"You think?" Susan felt dizzy so leant on the worktop. Jeffrey sniggered at her proving his point. She stood tall again. "If that's true, how come I'm the one who bailed us out when you blew the mortgage money on booze, stupid?"

Jeffrey shrugged.

"Say sorry for pissing in the kitchen."

"I didn't."

"Say. Sorry." Susan swayed as if her legs were about to go from under her. "Say sorry and promise never to do it again."

"I don't know what you're talking about."

Today's drink had made him cocky, spirits mixed with cola. She retched and stumbled towards the bathroom.

~

Susan handed Jeffrey a yellow pill.

"What do I need this for?"

"When you don't eat any fruit, you miss out on all the vitamins. We sat through a lecture about it last week and we're to try these with our families. They're free samples from the pharmaceutical company. The Sister said if we had to buy them ourselves they'd cost us a small fortune."

Susan put one in her mouth and took a sip of water then went to the bathroom. Jeffrey swallowed his with his cup of tea. In the bathroom Susan spat hers out and slipped it back in the brown glass container she'd earlier tipped it out of.

~

The doctor confirmed what Susan had guessed and assumed it was good news because of the gold ring on her finger.

"You're awfully skinny," he said. "Make sure you eat enough for two or the baby won't grow big enough. First child?" She nodded. "Well then, I'm sure your husband will be delighted."

"Pah."

Since getting married it was always the husband people mentioned first as if he was the most important one.

Rather than head home to share the news, Susan walked the streets trying to work out what to do with her new knowledge. Not a bug then, not the germs of another but rather the sperm of her husband, his stuff high up inside her, the thought of which made her gimp. It was all so messy and crude. She did not like it. She did not like that some of his gunk had defied gravity to impregnate her so soon into their marriage, not when she'd saved so little since buying the apartment and married mothers couldn't work. None that she knew earned their own money or got to enjoy the same freedoms their husbands did.

What to do.

What to do.

What to do without a second wage, with a child.

And what would the pregnancy do to her? Jeffrey would be alright, he wouldn't be affected whereas her belly would grow as her organs were squished. And what about her mind? Would she turn into that one? After years of running as far as she could would pregnancy drag her back with her mother's grip tight on her shoulders, flinging Susan into the heart of madness? No. Not if she didn't let it. Not if she got rid which she'd heard some girls did but that was dangerous. Her life was worth more than the risk of uncontrollable haemorrhaging.

Susan breathed out but not in again. What was the point of sucking up the air? She was a fool to think she could escape her past, it was still in her head no matter what she did. She remembered the mother, the father, the sister, the unit. If she made her family different would that mean she wasn't the same as her mother? If she created only one child rather than two then surely she wouldn't be like that woman which just left the money side of things to solve. Details. Mere details. She'd have a bath, work out how to sort it.

~

Susan handed Jeffrey an orange pill.

"Vitamin."

Susan handed him a yellow pill.

"Vitamin."

Susan handed him a green pill.

Susan handed him a pink pill.

"This one contains vitamins and minerals. They're new, meant to be even better than the yellow ones. They'd cost a fortune if we were having to pay for them ourselves. Aren't we just so lucky?"

~

On the way to the bathroom, Susan stepped in a pile of vomit. The edges of it were crusty, drying out in the heat. The yarn of the rug would be stained, the stupid idiot she'd married being too slow to make it to the bathroom. It wasn't that hard being sick, why couldn't he manage it? After red wine by the looks of it. He never drank red wine. No wonder he'd been ill, the stupid bloody idiot.

There was more vomit in the kitchen and chunks splattered all over the inside of the toilet bowl. He hadn't even bothered to flush it. Susan watched his comatose body from the doorway of the bedroom as it rose and fell under the covers. Why did he have to drink every night, waking up with a blurred head every morning? There wasn't an iota of discipline within his saggy, poisoned body, not poisoned enough, not even a hint of yellow to show his liver was turning bad. His organs, so far, were infallible.

She picked his suit jacket off the floor and put her hand into the inside pocket to take out what was left from his week's pay. She pulled out three receipts but no money. The largest cost was a meal for fifteen and the other two were bar tabs, all three of them from the same night. He'd spent the lot, a whole week's wages on his drinking buddies.

Susan kicked the side of the mattress. He juddered an inch then rolled back. She kicked it again and again: fool for spending the money, idiot for knowing nothing, smelly, dirty, stupid, drunk, boring pudgy fool, kick, fool, kick, fool, kick, fool, kick, fool, kick, fool, kick, kick kick kick. She could punch him in the face again and again, pulverising his cheekbone. He could see how his head hurt then, the god-damn idiot. She knelt by the bed and punched the side of the mattress instead, tears shoved back inside her eyes. He would not make her upset. He would not turn her weak. She refused to let him win. She would only be angry.

~

When Jeffrey went into the kitchen for breakfast, a cup of coffee and two slices of toast were waiting for him on the table.

"Can you come straight home from work tonight?"

"Why?"

"I need to talk to you." She smiled. "Please darling. I'm cooking your favourite."

~

Susan made Jeffrey a lasagne plus lemon cheesecake for dessert. As he sat down at the table, Jeffrey decided life was good and being married not so bad after all.

"Before we eat, I just need you to sign these papers."

"What are they?"

"Insurance."

"I thought we'd done that already."

"We did the life insurance but this is for here, the apartment, so the loan on it will be paid if I catch one of those fatal diseases at work. You know how dangerous it is, I told you my life expectancy's lower. And now we own a place, or part of it, what with me having saved up the deposit for the both of us, it would be a shame to lose it all because of God deciding I was needed for more important work in heaven. I mean, Samantha at work, she got stomach pains, nothing serious they thought then last week her husband brought her in all cramping and sweating, groaning at the agony. By yesterday morning she was dead. Only thirty four. Can you imagine? If something were to happen to me, what with all the germs I come into contact with Jeffrey… Well, I can't relax thinking you'd be left alone to pay for all of this or worse still, you'd fall behind with the payments and all that saving I did would have been for nothing with you thrown out on the streets by the bank, having to move back in with your parents. If you sign these forms, it'll all be paid for from the minute my heart stops beating."

"Jesus."

His belly rumbled.

"And life's different for us now. We need to plan ahead my darling."

He burped. "What are you talking about?"

"Didn't you notice the changes in me? We're going to have a baby."

Calton

Cal stepped off the bus in a town where the sun had beamed on his window as it parked in the bus station. He decided that was a good omen and there seemed to be enough buildings that he'd find work yet it was remote compared to a city, which was what he wanted and needed.

He grabbed the local paper from the stand in the empty ticket hall and a cold can of cola from the vending machine then sat on the beige steps near the door. There was only one job advertised that an unqualified person could do. It was at the morgue: someone to tag the bodies, complete basic paperwork, sit with the cold corpses through the day so they weren't all alone. They interviewed him that afternoon.

"Are you squeamish?"

"No."

"When are you able to start?"

"Tomorrow."

The only other applicant had stated in her interview that her mother made her apply. "Sorry but the thought of dead bodies creeps and freaks me out. I don't want to do it, not at all if that's okay with you but if you see my mother you have to tell her I turned up and did my best but simply wasn't suitable?"

They were desperate to fill the slot.

"I'm not scared of the dead," said Cal. "Both my parents died. I get it."

~

The bodies were stored beneath the street. A lift brought down the dead, stairs directed the living out. After the interview Cal walked up one flight of twenty seven steps. The intense sunshine made him falter. He would always put his sunglasses on before opening the door, play at being king vampire leaving his lair.

Having secured a wage he decided to splash out and buy lunch at a cafe. After weeks of scrimping, never eating more than two meals a day and only one of those filling, he ordered a plate of pancakes with maple syrup and freshly whipped cream. He sat for two hours, relishing them, feeling alternately full, tired, hungry again, determined not to leave until every scrap had been eaten. He smoked a cigarette outside. It felt good to have a job, to know he'd be earning money. When settling the bill he asked, "Do you know of any rooms to let?"

"As in a hotel, a shared house, a boarding house or—"

"A boarding house please."

A shared living space meant too many questions. His waitress called out to an older lady who was turning three burgers on the hot plate.

"Glenys. Glenys!" The lady turned to face them. "Do you know who might have space for a boarder at the moment? Gillian's full and—"

"Mrs Roth."

"Of course. Duh! Mrs Roth's your best bet. She lives a ten minute walk from here and is just lovely. She's been renting rooms out for years."

~

Cal settled into a routine: working, saving, eating and sleeping. Mrs Roth's gentle manner reminded him of his mother so he made sure he avoided her as much as he could. The only other lodger was an old man called Christopher. He and Mrs Roth played backgammon every evening and called out hello and goodbye without insisting that Cal stop and talk, which suited him perfectly.

The job was so quiet that on some days he felt guilty they were paying him to do so little. In the fourth week a seventh body appeared, Cal's seventh since starting. A male. When the doctor had finished her work, Cal did his, cleaning and labelling the body with the name found in the wallet that was still tucked into his trouser pocket after they scooped him out of the water.

That was his only work for the day. He sat and read for the other four hours, shoulders hunched, neck angled to the left, and when the reading made him dozy he lay down on one of the benches, placing his book under his head as a pillow.

Susan

Susan's mood switched from angry to sad so quickly that the shock of it made her sit down in the high backed arm chair she'd picked out in the shop for the support it gave her neck, no matter if it wasn't the latest fashion. She was glad it had arms that were raised as high as her waist, strong enough sides to support her as she pulled her knees up into her chest and stared at the carpet in front of her feet, not noticing daylight turn to dusk. Her hands were in her periphery vision. It was if they were pumping or throbbing, slightly out of focus. Even though she wanted to look at her fingers more closely she couldn't pull her eyes away from the staring they were doing, the staring at nothing while she felt so bloody sad. She'd rather have anger in charge of her.

At least Jeffrey was out so she could wallow in her maudlin thoughts except they weren't maudlin. They weren't anything. They were simply her stuck in a spot by a lack of feeling. How was that even possible, a doctor would ask, you're talking nonsense young lady, here dear, have some pills, the lilac ones, they're a favourite with all the house-wives. The doctor had never felt it so he didn't understand it. Rather than lilac pills what she needed was patience, time for the heaviness to lighten enough so it could float off her, which it would. It had before. Her nerve endings would start to care if they were alive or dead and remember to be receptive to what was around them. Her brain would gradually kick into action, reluctantly perhaps but refusing to give up. It would force her to be aware of where she was, who she was, that she had to get up out of the seat to cook dinner and go to work like a normal person.

She closed her eyes. Just for a minute she told herself, so glad that Jeffrey was out. She couldn't bear to have him hovering, asking if she was feeling alright, should he call a doctor as her behaviour was so out of sorts he was worried she was sickening for something serious and what about the baby. He would want to call his mother and NO Susan would have to shout, her neck jarring against the back of the chair.

No.

No-one should be called. She wanted no-one nor needed anyone. She would survive on her own as she was. That was the simplest solution, better for everyone, no need for under-qualified doctors with their medicines, the absolute bastards. There it was. She was okay. Bastardly god-damn freak of a bastard. There it was. There was the anger. That was better. She was alright now.

~

Susan showed Jeffrey a yellow, an orange and two red pills.

"Four a day from now on, that's what they've told us to take. We need to be extra careful to keep healthy. The red ones are full of minerals, good for your bones, that's what they say. I'll put them in your bag with your beer and potato chips. The orange one's got to be taken with food otherwise it'll make you shit the bed but if you make sure you have it after food's eaten you'll be fine. Don't forget now, not if you want to sleep next to me this evening."

~

Roger was already parked in the clearing when Jeffrey pulled up next to him, whistling as he got his fishing tackle and the cooler box out of the trunk. Jeffrey nearly ran down the river bank, clucking for a drink which was allowed because he was out with his friend and they would be celebrating and eleven in the morning was nearly midday so that was fine, nothing odd about that, no sir, absolutely no sir-ee-sir.

Once the camping chair was fixed firmly on the ground, Jeffrey opened his cooler box and found two bottles of wine next to his beers. He really was the luckiest. He'd married a good one, her bark was worse than her bite that was for sure. That's why she appeared so rude to people but if you knew her like he did, you'd realise that inside she was like a little puppy dog. He held a bottle up to show his friend.

"Some news. I'm going to be a father."

"Mate. Congratulations."

Roger grinned because now they had the best excuse to really go for it. They could drink until the edges weren't just blurred, that wasn't enough, they'd drink until they'd been blinded.

~

Wine and beer all gone, about to close the cooler box, Jeffrey remembered he had to swallow his pills. He laughed as he dropped the yellow one and watched it roll down the bank into the water, laughed at the knowledge that they'd invented pills to make a person super strong like in the movies. He managed to swallow the orange and the red ones. Good boy Jeffrey. As he and Roger stumbled up the hill, three steps up, one down, they laughed at their ineptitude, their tiredness from sitting, drinking, smoking for seven hours.

"See you Monday daddio."

Jeffrey looked at his friend's outstretched hand and missed when he tried to make his right one shake it. Roger cracked up.

"You're hilarious."

Jeffrey laughed, thrilled to have a fellow man think him funny rather than pathetic. And he was a man because never mind feeling a pair of titties, he'd sired a child which meant he was a true man who would leave a legacy. Roger reversed, waving his arm out of the car window as he drove off. Jeffrey watched him as he waved. The trees kept getting bigger and smaller. He shook the twisting picture out of his head and got in the car then went forwards rather than backwards, his foot hitting the brake when the front tyres were inches from going over the dusty bank.

"Shit," he laughed. "Christ's sake Jeffrey."

He span the car around, over steering to get onto the road, forgetting which side he was meant to be driving on. He tried to imagine a baby, the noises it would make. Jeffrey tried to imagine Susan as a mother but all he saw was her scowling which made no sense when he thought about it because she had all the same things his mother had so why was she so unhappy, so angry all of the time. Maybe it was because she needed the baby. That was it. That's what would make life better. His eyelids drooped. He shouldn't have had that last beer. Going fishing for the day was exhausting.

Susan

Susan was fifth in line at the bus stop when Sergeant Bray stood at the front of the queue.

"Mrs Jeffreys," he said.

She waited to see if it was another lady he was after.

"Is there a Susan Jeffreys here?"

She raised her left hand to shoulder height. Sergeant Bray made a face, not a grimace, not a smile, God knows what you'd call it, before he led her to the grassy area by the hospital's fountain that he'd scoped out on his arrival. He hoped the nurse would appreciate the privacy afforded by the seven foot high hedges that surrounded them.

~

After finding no-one home at the address listed in the wallet of the deceased, a long haired lady called Lola, from apartment 2B, had pointed Sergeant Bray in the direction of the hospital.

"I've seen her, the woman, the wife, wearing a nurse's uniform so I bet you she works at the hospital. She doesn't say much, never stops to chat. Is he in trouble or is it her? They seemed so nice, quiet, though he was always hiding his empties in the big bins outside so you never know. They've been here, what, two or three months I reckon. Has something happened? Some awful tragedy? Is that why you're looking for them?"

~

The nurses who could put a face to the name Mrs Jeffreys rushed around the wards searching for her until the Sister arrived back from her break and said Susan Jeffreys had finished her shift, would be making her way home by now. No, she didn't drive, she got the bus, they weren't sure which one, she had a husband, yes, no, sorry, none of them knew his name, the couple had only recently moved there. No, as far as they were aware they had no children, not yet anyway. She was a quiet one, efficient, one of the Sister's best and most reliable members of staff. Could she be of more help? Had something happened Officer?

~

Susan gripped her handbag tightly as the policeman told her the tragic news.

"There was a deep gash on Mr Jeffrey's forehead. He would have been unconscious when he drowned meaning there was no pain which is a comfort hopefully. The roads around here are hard enough to drive on if you know them, let alone if you're new to the area and I'm afraid Mr Jeffreys isn't the first to misjudge a bend, thinking he could take it at speed. There were tyre marks where he'd come off the road. Another driver saw him veering, flying... I'm so sorry Mrs Jeffreys. The Sister on the ward, she said you haven't lived here long. Is that right? The roads are particularly hard as dusk approaches especially if a person's had a drink. Is it possible your husband had been drinking Mrs Jeffreys?"

"Why do you ask?"

"Well—"

"Oh, what does it matter now? Yes. I'm afraid it is Officer."

She didn't cry. The Sergeant wrongly assumed it was because she was as used to death as he was, considering her line of work. Or the shock of it. The shock of a close one dying unexpectedly often did strange things to people.

He drove her home and as they climbed the stairs to her apartment they could hear the phone ringing. It stopped when they reached the landing on the second floor but as soon as she opened her front door, it started again. Susan answered it. Let the gossiping begin then she'd unplug it from the socket.

"My husband is dead," she said, as if it was the dullest news there could be. Sister Cunniffe told her to take as much time off as she needed and Susan was to let them know if she wanted help with anything, anything at all, she really meant it and she'd make sure Susan kept being paid of course. She wasn't to worry about a thing, not a thing, the far too young to be widowed poor darling.

"Would you like me to fetch someone?" asked Sergeant Bray.

Susan shook her head.

"I can call someone to sit with you, or if you'd rather, an officer can go with you to help tell his family."

"Where's his body?"

"At the morgue on Hollybush Road, near the hospital. They'll keep it there until they move it to the funeral home. There's some information in this leaflet and a number you can call if you have any questions." When she didn't hold out her hand, he laid the yellow pamphlet on the pale wooden coffee table. "It—"

"You can go now."

After the front door had clicked shut, Susan sat at the ash desk in the corner of the living room and scrambled through the drawers searching for a copy of Jeffrey's new job's life insurance forms. She already knew the figures for the mortgage and the joint life insurance. The paperwork was missing. The messy fool hadn't filed it properly. She'd have to visit his office to find out what she was due from the council but first, she needed to see him, to have proof he really was gone. The leaflet said the coroner's office opened at 11am on Monday.

~

Roger was sprawled on the ground outside the main entrance to the apartment like a beggar in a bigger town. He was drunk. Drunk as always and thinking that was a better state to be in than sober which it wasn't, not to anyone except him, not even him if only he'd realise, the stupid bloody drunkard.

"Susan," he wailed. "Such terrible news. Awful. He was my best buddie." He hugged her. She recoiled from the smell of alcohol on his breath and slipped out of his grip so her back was against the apartment wall. He looked at her expectantly but she did not invite him in.

"Such sad news," he blubbed. "I couldn't believe it when they told me. I walked out of the office, shock I think. I mean I'd wondered why he hadn't come in today but I never thought... I can't believe it. He was too young, it's too tragic." She wished she smoked. This was where she'd light a cigarette. It would be handy to have a reason to appear distracted, have a reason to look anywhere except at the pathetic man's rosy, puffed up features. "How are you doing? It must be awful being widowed so young. Too bloody young I tell you." He pointed at her as he shook his head before glugging down half of the beer in his hand. "And the baby. You and the baby all alone now. He was so excited about becoming a daddio."

"We lost the baby. There's no need for you to be worried about that."

"What? Oh no," he cried. "More tragedy. You've lost the both of them. God bless you but it's a cruel world."

Tears spewed as his shoulders shook. Susan took a deep breath as she worked out how best to deal with him.

"Was he drinking all day? The police want to know." Roger grimaced. "Don't worry, I won't tell them. I just want to know for me, so I know what happened. I told him not to drink so much, begged him not to drink and drive but if he did, if he'd had a load of beer, in lots of ways that would be a comfort as then I'd know he hadn't been in pain, that he'd have been all relaxed when he drove into the water. The wine was missing, from our wedding, the last two bottles that I'd been keeping to wet the baby's head, but when I looked in the fridge this morning I noticed they were gone."

"He said you gave them to him. He said you didn't mind about the drinking."

"He can't have."

"He did. He said you were okay with it, with him having a few beers, that you were the best wife a man could hope for because of the leniency and the love and look at you even making sure he had his vitamins."

Susan's head flicked to the side as if she'd been shoved. She gave her practised look of pain.

"How could he have done that? Did he not think before he got in the car, before he drove back on those windy roads, that it was his life he was playing with, and what about the lives of all those who were joined to him? I hope you don't drink and drive Roger."

"I begged him not to."

"Really?"

He started crying again. "I should go. You'll tell me when the funeral is?"

"Of course."

"You're so kind. I—"

"There's no baby though. Make sure you remember that. Jeffrey's brain must have been so addled with grief that he forgot to tell you or perhaps he was in denial after wanting it so badly." Susan raised her hand to her mouth. "He wouldn't have done it on purpose? He wouldn't have driven into the river at speed because he was so sad at the loss of his child?" She whipped up the water behind her eyes and wiped her cheeks as if it was escaping. "No. It was the drink, the drinking and the driving, that's what got him, it has to be. I used to say to him, Jeffrey it'll be the death of you. But I didn't want that to come true Roger. I didn't mean it."

The Meeting

Cal put his sunglasses on and opened the heavy, metal door onto the street that was as quiet as the catacomb he was leaving behind. A figure stepped in front of him. The door halted his backwards stumble. The pale lady stared at him. The thought of her being some weird living dead ghost thing flickered into his head. He chastised himself.

"Are you okay?" he asked. "Miss?"

Cal didn't know what else to do so remained awkwardly wedged between her and the door. Time ticked forward as they both stood still. He checked his watch and looked anxiously down the road as if he was about to miss a bus.

"I'm sorry but I have to go now," he said.

"Just a look," Susan mumbled.

"Excuse me?"

"Can I see him?"

"Him?"

"Yes."

Cal felt like he was back in school, not knowing the answer to a question in class, too scared to speak in case he got it wrong and the teacher got cross, desperately wishing he knew the right thing to say.

"My husband's body. It was brought in at the weekend. Please."

That was against the rules. They'd emphasised it at his induction. But she looked so sad and lost, like his Dad had after Cal's Mum had died.

"Alright. Just for a second. You mustn't tell anyone though?"

She nodded. He led her down the stairs, his stomach cramping with nervousness. Susan held her hand to her nose to dilute the smell of disinfectant. Working there had made Cal immune to the strength of it. He remembered the man's name and decided to check hers in case she was an imposter, up to no good.

"And the name is?"

"Jeffreys." Her eyes scanned the cupboards behind him.

"First name?"

"Is there more than one dead Jeffreys here today?"

He felt like a child, caught out at playing a worker.

"So you'd like to see the body of Jason Jeffreys?"

"Jeffrey Jeffreys. You know it's not Jason."

Her lips turned down like a sad clown and Cal felt ashamed. He opened the door to pull out the metal shelf. The man's naked body embarrassed him, even though it was her husband. He expected her to recoil but instead she moved cautiously along the edge of the body, never taking her eyes off it as if he might come alive. The shelf was as high as her neck and when she bent down to sniff, her nose nearly glanced off her husband's arm. She reached up to stroke his belly but after a brief touch withdrew her hand.

"He's freezing."

She studied her husband as if trying to work out why

he was there, how they'd both ended up in this unfamiliar room. She started to whisper in his ear. Cal moved further away to give them some privacy.

"Drunken idiot." She poked her husband's arm sharply with her index finger. "Now I'll be all alone to care for it." She punched his arm then started to cry. Cal thought she was getting a tissue from her bag but instead she took out a camera and held it up. "Smile." Press and wind on, press and wind on. The flash popped extra light around the room.

"I'm not sure you're allowed to do that."

Cal jumped forward. She took a picture of him.

"No-one will know."

Susan turned her back on the boy and the body, climbed the stairs and left the building. Relieved, Cal swooshed the shelf back in its tomb, ran up the stairs and cautiously opened the door. Sure that she was gone, he sprinted to his lodgings.

Mrs Roth and Christopher were playing backgammon, the sun shining through the living room window, into her eyes. Cal called out *hey* as he ran up the stairs, straight to his bedroom where he rolled a strong spliff, half tobacco/half weed which he smoked on the flat roof outside his window. It helped him sleep with no dreams and no memories. He folded up the fact that it was his mother and father's wedding anniversary and hid it deep down in his brain.

~

Three bodies were crushed in a car crash. That meant the police, pathologist, priest and undertaker all visited. They sighed, tutted, nodded and shook their heads. Cal helped

187

as best he could and was praised for good work son. Three bodies were tucked away leaving two families grieving, frantically trying to work out what had happened to their world, wishing they could turn the clock back twenty four hours. Cal triple cleaned the benches and sterilised the tools. He double checked the room. After all the bustling, it was so still he held his breath so he didn't disturb the peace. He turned the lights off and wearily climbed the stairs, glad they'd told him he could leave early.

Sunglasses on, Cal stepped out to join the living. A young mother was pushing a red pram. He let her pass and they smiled at one another. The world was still turning. Sometimes, when he was down below, he imagined opening the door and it had all gone, the earth disappeared so he stepped straight into space and floated towards the stars.

The morning had worn him out. He had a familiar feeling; he wouldn't last much longer in this town. The deaths were too sad and complicated for him. He needed to march on, be around positivity.

A hand clamped onto his shoulder.

It didn't tentatively tap but stayed firmly an inch from his neck. He looked down and to the right. Elegant fingers with clean, white tips were resting on his collar bone. As he turned, Mrs Jeffreys lowered her arm.

"You're early. You look tired though. Bad day?"

"It was pretty awful."

Susan nodded like she knew what he meant. Her empathy made him talk as they walked: cleaning the broken bodies, trying to hide the nasty wounds from the parents, wishing fervently that he could have been anywhere but there. When he finished and looked up, Cal realised he was in a part of town he didn't know, in front of a three storey bright, white apartment block.

"Would you like a drink?"

It felt rude not to.

The communal hallway was pale green with a large cacti by the cubby holes for post. An unwelcoming plant, in Cal's opinion. The widow lived on the top floor. When she opened the door the green ended and pure white walls welcomed them. She'd left all the windows open and it smelt as fresh as the freesias in the glass vase on her mantelpiece.

She poured her guest a large shot of whiskey. It burned his throat but he needed the kick to rid himself of sad thoughts. Susan stared at his torso, so much skinnier than her husband's pudgy frame. She preferred it.

She emptied her glass faster than him and as soon as he'd finished his drink she grabbed his glass, took it to the kitchen and came back with both re-filled to the top. Cal wasn't used to spirits. It created a different edge to the smoking. He picked at a loose thread on his t-shirt.

"I should go now."

She sat next to him on the navy sofa. "It's been a very bad week—"

"Sure."

Susan bit her lip. She didn't like being interrupted. Cal downed the rest of the amber liquid and slammed the glass on the coffee table harder than he meant to, making his host jump.

"Sorry. I'd better go."

"No."

She placed her hand on his thigh. He jerked in response. Her hand moved down and across his leg so close to his crotch that her little finger touched the zip on his trousers. He didn't move himself or her hand. He pushed his hands onto the sofa to rise but she pushed firmly on his groin and with the other hand undid his belt. They didn't kiss. She didn't even take off her dress. His watch got caught in her stockings so she unclasped it and dropped it on the floor. He gave in with a groan so loud a lady walking her dog looked up at the open window and considered calling an ambulance in case someone had been taken ill. When the noise stopped she decided not to cause a fuss and carried on, pulling Snappy by his lead.

In the white room Cal's head cleared of the drink. His hip hurt so he moved to the left and Susan immediately pulled herself off him. The skirt of her dress was so long he'd not even seen her thighs. He was embarrassed by the gunk that dripped onto her sofa. He wiped it with his hand. Although that made the stain flatter it was wider and to him, all the more obvious. He moved his right buttock to sit on it and felt the moistness through his trousers. When he stood up, there'd be a wet patch on them too.

"I should go."

He pulled up his zip. She looked like she was going to cry. He waited for her to speak and closed his eyes as he tried to make a decision. He needed a smoke.

"I'll go."

Once she heard the front door close Susan went into the bedroom and pulled a cardboard box from under the bed. She took off the soft, pale blue blanket that lay on top of it and pulled out two matching frames. One contained the picture of her and Jeffrey on the night he'd proposed, the other a picture of them on their wedding day.

They were both smiling, sort of. She picked out a third frame that matched the first two, a gift from her mother-in-law for the future, for a photo of grandchildren. Anger overwhelmed sadness. Susan ran a bath so hot that it turned her skin a glowing red the minute it was submerged. She viciously massaged her belly, willing the filling away, wondering what the name of the morgue boy was. If there was a heaven Jeffrey might be watching, sickened by his wife fornicating when he wasn't even buried, discussing with God how best to punish her.

"It's your fault you drunkard," she shouted. "I am not to blame!"

The Watch

Cal wasn't sure if he'd been used or if he'd used her. He ran. It made sense to physically run away, the further he got the less of an issue it would be. He passed apartment blocks with pristine lawns and flowers in full bloom. He sprinted over clean, grey pavements and across pale beige roads using his finely tuned sense of direction from months on the road. He passed a familiar square of grass kept for child's play then a green telephone box on a corner and finally, the road near work that meant he was near his room. When he reached the boarding house he shouted out *hey* in the hallway and ran up the stairs to his bedroom, locking the door behind him.

Lungs bursting, he got his tin from the back of the top drawer, unravelling the jumper he'd hidden it in. He rolled a spliff and inhaled with breath he hadn't quite caught. His lungs protested. They were working hard enough trying to get oxygen all around without fumes getting in the way but they backed down as his breathing regulated and his nervousness eased. He pulled up the sash of his window but didn't climb onto the roof. Instead, he leant over the sill and smoked until there was half a centimetre left. He ran the soggy stub under the tap in his room to make sure it was out, folded it in paper and put it in the bin. Then he worried it was still burning so took the paper out of the bin, tapped the stub onto his palm and rubbed it between his fingers until a few shreds of plant and paper were left. After washing his hands, he relaxed. There'd be no house fire from his smoking. He worried about the wiring. The switches were old, who knew how safe it was. He poked his head out of the window and took a deep breath of warm air. It smelled sweetly of the honeysuckle growing on the roof garden of the house next door.

How had she known what time he finished work? Had she been watching him, in which case it must be him who'd been used? She might be watching now. He shut the window, screwed the bolt and pulled down the blind. He peed in the sink rather than leave the room and although part of him knew it was ridiculous, he put one of his pillows in front of the door to give him some warning if she or anyone else tried to break in. He peed in the sink again. Only a dribble came out though Cal had felt like he was busting to go. He splashed water all around it so he wasn't completely foul and hoped his mother wasn't in heaven shaking her head, tutting at his behaviour. Correction. He hoped his mother was in heaven, should it exist, but not seeing him piss in a sink. There was no need for her to witness that. He crawled under his blankets and moved the pillow under his head. As he stared at the ceiling, blanket all the way to his neck not letting any demons in, he remembered the feel of Mrs Jeffreys and was ashamed. He'd left her all alone, too upset to even speak. What he'd done was wrong. He should re-trace his steps and visit her. He persuaded himself that's what he would do and conscience eased, fell asleep.

~

Susan played with the watch the boy had left behind. She would call him the boy even though he was an adult. But he was so young. He was disturbed deep down, she could tell. It should be easy enough to get him to do what she wanted.

She felt no guilt at having done it with another man when her husband wasn't buried yet and she felt no sadness that Jeffrey had died because he was a fool. She was finding there were a lot of fools, both arrogant and stupid, and Jeffrey had been one of them and the planet was better off without him, one less mouth for its fields to feed. The child would be better off without him too because he'd have been a soft touch of a father, easily manipulated by its whinging and demands, she was sure of it. He'd have spoilt it, over-feeding his little darling with lemon cheesecake, making it all rotund and as the mother, the wife, she'd be the one who got the blame, who'd have to shoulder the judgemental stares of other parents.

It made her so angry, the thought of how Jeffrey might have behaved if he were alive. And the fact that she couldn't get rid of the anger made her furious. Were others always so cross? It didn't look like it, didn't seem to be the case, not all the time at least, not like she was. Every night there'd be a brief moment where she'd wonder when she woke up would she be smiling like people she saw in the shops, the bank, the street, on their way to church on a Sunday. But at sunrise her mouth would always be clenched, the left side of her jaw aching from the teeth that had been grinding throughout the night, her fingers sore where they'd clawed the sheets in her sleep rather than relaxing.

She put the watch in her handbag and headed out. She

knew where he worked, where he ate, where he slept at night. She would return it to him.

~

Cal woke to silence and darkness though he couldn't remember turning off the light. He fumbled in the gloom for his watch but it wasn't in its usual spot. That flummoxed him. He always laid it beside him when he slept. He turned on the main light, checked the floor, the dresser, his jacket and the pockets of his trousers. He felt a stiff stain on the crotch and remembered the watch getting caught. In his rush to escape he'd forgotten to grab it. He cursed the whole, stupid afternoon.

He peeked under the blind. The sun was low in the sky, it was too early for work. He ran a bath, keeping the door shut so he didn't disturb Mrs Roth. She was such a lovely. That was what his mother used to call good people. Her voice would sing as she spoke. He missed the sound of A to C to D.

The bath was deep and hot, the soap the cheapest one the local store stocked. He rubbed it all over his body, missing out only the centre of his back. He tried to wash off the previous day but after vigorously drying himself the shame still clung to him.

When his stomach rumbled he knew the half a loaf of bread in the wire cupboard in the far corner of the room wouldn't satisfy his hunger. He pulled out a blue tin from inside a grey jumper that was under a white t-shirt in his deepest drawer. It contained enough money for breakfast and after another pay cheque, a ticket to travel on. He took out two notes, re-hid the tin and leaving the blind down, left the house.

It felt wise to be out so early. The air smelt fresher and the streets were empty except for him and the birds twittering on and on. He reached 'Eat, drink' before it was open so sat on the curb to prepare for the uncertain day ahead. He had to find the widow's apartment and retrieve his watch. Simple. No need to be so anxious.

"Feel the vibe?"

"Pardon?"

Glenys didn't reply. The noise of the keys was louder than his voice and her mind was on the water to boil, eggs to crack, bacon to fry. Cal wasn't sure of the etiquette for arriving too early, whether he could follow her straight in or should he wait until the door sign was turned round, permitting customers to cross the threshold?

"Come on then," she snarled. They would be busy within the hour. Cal's stomach rumbled as the door shut behind him. "You'll have to wait while I sort everything out."

He sat quietly in a booth as she chopped mushrooms, beat batter in a silver bowl and poured coffee beans in the percolator. Her face hardened when she looked at him. She was a little jealous of his youth and freedom, unaware of his loss.

"Do you know what you want?"

"The number seven please, and a coffee."

She put a wedge of butter on the griddle. The smell of it melting made his mouth moisten so much he had to swallow.

Cassandra walked in, surprised to see Glenys already serving the morgue boy. There was something about him. That's what they said, the women who'd waited behind him in a queue or had a parent die so whispered conspiratorially, shamefully, when drunk on wine at the funeral.

Those eyes, those cheekbones.

Glenys nodded towards the coffee. Cassandra hung up her cardigan. Though it was a hot summer she always took one out with her. Her boyfriend said she'd wear one in the middle of a nuclear attack and although the joke had worn thin, she still laughed when he said it because she loved him. She poured Cal a coffee.

"You feel the vibe?" she asked.

"Excuse me?"

"That's what I said to him," said Glenys.

"Haven't seen you in days and now you're here?" He still didn't get it. She pinged open the till. "For you."

She put his watch on the table. He choked on a mouthful of bacon, swallowed and coughed again.

"A lady came in yesterday at closing time, asked if we could pass it on."

The way he strapped it to his wrist, they could see it was worth a lot to him.

"Thank you."

Cassandra hovered, hoping for some of the story, how the lady had come to have it. She hadn't ordered food or drink so they couldn't tell anything about her from that. Her clothes had been plain but her hair was long, dark and luscious. It shone which meant she ate well.

"Morning ladies."

Merlin took his usual seat, having left his dog tied up outside.

Cassandra smiled at the old man and poured him a black coffee, putting three sugars on the saucer before taking it over. Cal took his cup outside to enjoy a rolled up cigarette in the fresh air. The wizard's dog eyed him lazily then closed his eyes and farted. Cal shifted along the step to escape the putrid smell, checked his watch and decided he had time for another coffee as re-fills were paid for from the first sip. Cassandra was busy with a third set of customers, two construction workers, so he waited until she passed his table before holding up his cup.

"Did she say anything?"

"No." Cassandra was now desperate to know more. "Were you expecting her to? Wish you had her number?" He didn't return her smile. "I'm sure she'll be back."

Cal shrugged, apparently not caring. He drank slowly, checking the time, feeling the watch with his fingertips. When nine o'clock came he paid, leaving a larger tip than usual for the early service, their safe keeping of his watch, and the large portion of food.

"Thank you," he called.

Glenys nodded her head to acknowledge him but didn't turn from the omelette she was flipping.

~

In his room that evening Cal got out a map of the bus routes. It was his favourite bit, choosing a new town to visit, a new road to travel. The country opened up before him as he spread the map out on the floor. He would check ticket prices and work out how far he could afford to go with what he'd saved so far. When his stomach rumbled for a third time he folded the map exactly along its creases and filed it carefully away. Never eat, drink or smoke over a map. That's what his father had taught him.

~

Now Cal had made his mind up to resign he wanted to say the words out loud to make it real. He checked the stairs, listened out for the lift, opened two drawers half way and stood between Mr Elios and Dr Neru.

"I'm afraid I have to leave. You made me feel such a valued member of your team but it's time for me to move on."

He bowed before shutting them back in, closing the doors simultaneously as he mouthed the words rest in peace.

By the end of the day a dull ache throbbed persistently above his right eyebrow, too much time spent reading in the unnatural light. He put his sunglasses on as he left the building.

"Hello."

Three times she'd made him jump. Susan looked down, increasing the awkwardness even though it was her who'd made the next move.

"Thanks for my watch." Cal raised his left arm to show her he was wearing it. "I hadn't been there in a while. Funny you knew to take it there."

She looked at him so intently he turned his head away, pretending to watch someone across the street. She obviously wasn't going to move on and he was too polite, too cowardly, to leave her by herself again. He fiddled with his sunglasses.

"I'm going that way," he said.

"Me too."

They walked towards the bus station, not touching, not speaking. If she got too close he shifted his weight to the right, stepping so near the wall that he scraped his elbow on the brick. The blood bubbled and coagulated, creating the beginnings of a scab.

"Are you feeling better?" he asked. "I know it's early days but—"

"A little."

She slipped her hand in his, mistaking politeness for caring. Cal resisted the urge to pull away while also wishing he was naturally callous. He tried to distance himself.

"How are the funeral arrangements going?"

"It'll be quiet. Only myself and some of his colleagues from work. You're welcome to come."

He let go of her hand to itch his eyebrow.

"I didn't know him."

"You know me."

"A little."

"Intimately."

Cal stopped walking and spoke firmly, trying to copy the tone his father would have used when asserting authority over his young son.

"I really don't think that would be appropriate." He looked at his watch. "I have to get going now. You have a good evening Ma'am."

Susan pushed her thumbnail into her index finger as she watched him walk away from her. She'd been abandoned, second time in a week. Her eyes hardened. It wasn't good enough. At home she grabbed the vodka from the fridge, downed a glass and examined her stomach. It had always been flat and taut but now it was swollen, matching her heavier breasts, even sorer this week than last. The changes were imperceptible to anyone else but she knew her skirts were tighter, that her pants hugged closer and itched in the heat. She'd bought a new bra before Jeffrey had died and now wished she'd chosen a bigger cup size. Such a waste. Such an annoyance.

The Sickness

Susan threw up in the white toilet bowl then carefully wiped the rim and put the seat back down. After she'd flushed, streaks of vomit still floated in the basin. Her hand reached out to flush again when a fresh surge of nausea swept through her. This set was more violent. She had to catch her breath afterwards.

Her legs wobbled as she sat on the bed. If it wasn't for the baby she'd feel satisfied with life but pregnancy mixed with widowhood had made the inheritance more complicated. She knew right from wrong, that she should tell Jeffrey's parents about their grandchild as well as their son's death, they may even pay towards raising it. But the thought of eighteen years of interference and contact made her shiver so much a cold sweat formed on her brow. She needed to sell the apartment and move even further away from them, thousands of miles rather than hundreds.

Her heart was beating too fast, her head felt light. She pushed her hand on her belly, wishing the foetus would shrivel up and die but no pain came, no blood, no fairy godmother appeared to empty her womb.

She took out the appointment sheet with the due date that she'd hidden between the pages of her Greys Anatomy book. No love leapt from her heart to the thin piece of white paper that curled its edges between her cold fingers. A new wave of sickness came. She made it to the bathroom but some bits splattered on her feet. She scrunched the paper up and threw it in the toilet bowl. After flushing twice it bobbed up again, determined to survive. Susan pissed on it and flushed the chain before returning to bed. Jeffrey zig–zagged though her mind. In the bathroom the soggy paper floated wearily on the surface of the water.

~

Susan arrived fifteen minutes early at the undertaker's. She picked up a coffin brochure from the table in the reception area. Best buy the cheapest one, it was only going to be burnt. They gave her a leaflet for the local hotel they recommended for receptions. All its rooms had verandas, for those who needed air. The manager spoke calmly, his low voice confident and kind.

"And the family can travel in cars behind the hearse, immediate family, parents, sisters, brothers, whoever you choose."

"There's just me."

"One car then."

"Is it expensive? Can't I travel up front?"

"I'm sorry?"

"With you, in the hearse. It'd save a whole car being wasted on just me."

In twenty seven years Mr Grade had never been asked by a relative if they could sit up front, nor to his knowledge had his father or his father's father. People usually wanted distance from the coffin until the very end where they might throw themselves on the lid.

He pondered upon her request. Business was constant, their monopoly fruitful. The navy, velvet chairs they'd recently bought looked smart against the cream carpet and freshly painted magnolia walls. His secretary, Patricia, was right to choose navy rather than the green he'd suggested.

"It can't be green," she said. "There's nothing lucky about death unless the will is generous."

This widow mustn't have any money. She was a thin thing. It couldn't be easy paying for a funeral and having enough left for rent and decent food.

"That will be fine," he said.

~

The bank manager shook her hand. Susan tilted her head to the right in acknowledgment. There were no other customers. The tellers stared at her from behind their counter. Mr Simmons held out his arms and gave her a *bless you* look before leading her to his office. Susan sat opposite him.

"I'm so sorry for your loss."

"He's not lost, he's dead. How much do I get?"

"Excuse me?"

"I've seen Jeffrey's last statement but he should have been paid on Friday. Did he drop any cash into his account that afternoon?"

Mr Simmons was used to all sorts sitting across his desk: builders begging for more, husbands asking for secret loans, a wife questioning the accuracy of a settlement. But no widow or widower had been so blatant, stared him in the face and asked how much. He excused her because of the baby bump. His wife had also been crazy at that particular time. It's as if she's speaking Chinese, he used to tell his golf buddies. Mrs Jeffreys made the hairs on his neck rise up, made him wary. He opened the file.

"Was there life insurance?"

"Yes. Plus he worked for the council."

"There'll be a good policy there then. The details are probably with your solicitors or their personnel department."

"I'm visiting Hardle and Carew's after this."

"Excellent. I play squash with Hardle's son. He's a great guy, studied law but went into journalism then..." She was the sort of woman that made you want to fill a silence. "I can call them on your behalf if you'd prefer, to help you sort everything out."

"At a cost."

"Excuse me?"

"Do I need to sign anything?"

"You will."

"Do I need to write letters?"

"H & C can do that for you."

"Charging a fee for each one."

"A nominal fee. It's standard practice. Look, you must be exhausted in your condition. I recommend you accept help where it's available."

Her eyes widened a fraction. He was the first person to notice.

"Pah." She folded her arms across her stomach.

"Mrs Jeffreys, I know the company and I know their staff. They're an honest firm."

"Anything else?"

"Whatever we can do to—"

"Answer my questions."

"Certainly." His tone was now clipped to match hers. "Do you have a copy of the death certificate?"

"Yes.

"We can contact you on this number?"

"Yes."

"That's all we need for now then."

~

The apartment was too bright. Four o'clock sun glared through the windows. Susan pulled down the blackout blinds. Jeffrey had offered more money so she could buy something prettier, like the flowery curtains his mother hung in every room. How little he knew her.

The meeting with the solicitors had gone well. Mr Carew told her there was Jeffrey's life insurance as well as the policy they'd taken out to cover the mortgage plus a widow's pension and lump sum from his workplace. She'd be fine financially, some would say very well off indeed. She checked her watch. The morgue boy would finish his shift in five minutes which didn't leave her enough time to get to him. She could go to his rooms but that was likely to spook him. Would he take on a woman and child? She wouldn't. If the roles were reversed she'd refuse to play the part of stepmother but maybe he'd be kinder. It wasn't born yet, that had to make it easier to pretend, for her and him though now they'd done the deed she could say it was his baby. Not yet. That might scare him off. She'd keep it secret for a month, maybe two, or until it was born, that would be the best thing, keep an element of surprise and all that. There was a ward nurse who'd told her boyfriend too soon and she'd ended up on her own. Then she got depressed and cried all the time, even at work. Her parents came for her. Heads down, no words of comfort, drops of disappointment from the mother swallowed by a steely stare of disapproval from the father. Susan had glared at him. It wasn't fair. Just because she was a girl she had to carry the burden whilst the boy ran away and lived his life, not caring or changing one single thing. She'd sworn if a boy did that to her she'd follow him and mortify him, make him play a part in the upbringing.

Susan would be patient and visit the morgue the next day with her legitimate excuse. Mr Grade had said yes to her offer to deliver the clothes there to dress the body, even though the casket would be a closed one.

"His best suit?" she'd asked.

"Not necessarily. It's not a job interview."

"Unless he meets God and the devil and has to persuade them which path he should take."

"I'm sure it's upwards."

"Maybe. Does God love a drinker?"

"Isn't he meant to love everyone?"

"I don't know. I've never met him so can't tell. What do you think?"

Mr Grade guessed that she wouldn't mind his atheism. He'd never told anyone; his family certainly wouldn't understand. He used the hours spent sitting inside and waiting outside churches to solve complicated mathematical sums rather than pray. Clients generally grasped onto the afterlife though in his opinion that prolonged and enhanced their pain. This lady was different.

"I don't suppose it matters."

"His favourite clothes?"

"Yes."

"He didn't really care about clothes."

"Whatever you choose will be fine. It's only going to be burnt."

"Yes. Exactly. That's exactly right. It is isn't it?"

She'd bring his cheapest trousers and shirt. No-one would know. Was everyone naked in the afterlife? The thought of all those bare bodies disgusted her. She decided not. It would be too ugly.

~

Susan held out a white paper bag from the hospital. Cal was trapped. He stood behind the stool, brain undecided on whether to fight or flee. They used the white bags to hand over the belongings of people who'd died unexpectedly: crash deaths, heart failures, the victims of violent crime. Patients with advance warning of a stay always had their own bags.

"These are his clothes for the funeral. Not his best. Mr Grade at the funeral parlour, he told me to bring them here."

Cal wanted to lock up. He was meeting Thomas, his supplier of weed, a man who wouldn't wait. Cal had placed a special order to help him get to sleep which he'd been finding difficult since meeting the widow.

"They usually dress them at the funeral parlour."

"Well he said to bring the clothes here. Check if you like."

Why was there no bell on the door? It was too easy for her to open it up and walk right in. There was nowhere for Cal to hide and he'd had no warning she was coming until he heard her feet on the steps. It made him too vulnerable.

He accepted the bag and put it on a bench. It looked like a still life waiting to be painted in a college art class.

The creases went at odd angles with a bump where some socks stuck out, like the widow's tummy. A small mound sat below her ribs, imperceptible to anyone who hadn't taken notice of how skinny she was before. Cal could see the difference.

"You can go now."

She scowled before stomping up the stairs.

~

"Mr Carew. It's Mrs Jeffreys. I'd like to sell the apartment. Immediately. What do I need to do to make that happen?"

Sidney Carew's mind whirred as he scratched his bald head. He'd been on the lookout for an apartment in that area for the past year. How best to get a good deal and assure her they could both emerge as winners.

"Mr Carew?"

"Yes, sorry, some people outside, acting odd. So, you want to sell your apartment?"

"Yes."

"Have you had it valued?"

"No."

"Spoken to an agent?"

"Not yet."

"Right. Well, the best thing is for you to come in and we can talk through the procedures involved. Have you seen another apartment you'd like to buy?"

"I'm just selling, moving away."

"Excellent. That makes it less complicated."

"How long will it take?"

"That depends on the price, finding a buyer, it can be tricky in today's market."

"I'll call an agent this afternoon."

"No need to rush."

"Yes there is. I want to sell it as soon as possible."

"Right you are." Sidney scratched his nose as he thought about how best to phrase it. "I'll be honest with you Mrs Jeffreys. I've been looking for an apartment in that area for a couple of months now. My sister is recently divorced from a very unhappy marriage and she could do with a nice place to live. Between you and me, she's feeling very low."

"Better than being widowed."

Sidney paused. "Indeed. I'd pay a fair price."

"I'm not a fool Mr Carew."

"Oh, I'm aware of that Mrs Jeffreys."

"Will it be fast?"

"Absolutely."

"Six weeks, five weeks, four weeks—"

"Mrs—"

"–three weeks, two weeks, one week."

Sidney laughed. "Like I said, I'll do my best."

Susan had him. This could be good. No middle men creaming off a profit for doing nothing, no need to chase paperwork between all the solicitors' offices. He'd make sure it all moved as quick as can be.

"One week and it's yours."

"That's impossible."

"One week."

"I'll try."

"One week or it goes to the first cash buyer."

"We'll need to agree a price."

"I'll call you back with a figure."

He gave her his home phone number.

The Hiding

Susan let the telephone ring, ring, ring and when it eventually stopped, she unplugged it. It would be Jeffrey's mother. He used to speak to her every Sunday, after a bottle of wine, once he was relaxed and not quite himself.

~

Jane gave up and put the receiver down. She fretted. They'd exchanged no news for ten whole days.

"Something's not right."

"You said that already," her husband replied.

"I know my Jeffrey. You know Jeffrey. Something's not right."

She phoned her sister.

"He's still not answering."

"Really? Something's not right."

"That's what I said. John thinks I'm over-reacting, I can tell."

"Ignore him. You know what he's like."

Jane heard the click of a cigarette lighter.

"I thought you'd given up."

"Cut down."

"You said—"

"So, do you think she's buried the body?"

"Don't say that. My god Miriam, I can't believe you just said that."

"I'm joking, just trying to lighten the mood. Christ."

"Where is he then?"

"Did you have a row?"

"No! We never row. It's her, getting her evil claws into him. What should I do?"

"Keep calling."

"There's no point. It's never answered."

"Maybe there's a problem with the line?"

"I've checked three times already."

"Then go visit."

"You think?"

"Definitely. A surprise visit. Bring some things from his room. Say you need the cupboard space."

"No."

Jane had kept Jeffrey's room exactly as he'd left it, in the hope that he might come back one day.

"What about a house warming present then? You said they've bought the apartment?"

"Yes."

"But you've never been?"

"No."

"Do that then. I'll come with you."

"Really?"

"Absolutely. For support."

"What about John?"

"What about him?"

"I should tell him."

"But if he doesn't want to go, count me in. She's a strange one I tell you, a bit crazy. Hey, don't cry. Awww, come on.

It'll be okay. He's a grown man isn't he? And the phone company might have got it wrong you know. Remember when I moved into Clement Street, it took nine weeks to get the line sorted and they kept telling me it was working fine."

"They did, didn't they?" Jane sniffed.

"See. There'll be some simple explanation."

"You're right. I'm being silly." She sniffed again. "God, I miss him so much."

"I know. Why don't we go on Saturday?"

"This Saturday?"

"Buy them a present and off we go."

"Right. You're right. I'll buy one tomorrow."

"And call me if you hear anything."

John was dozing in the forest green, corduroy chair her parents had bought them as a wedding present. She called his name. He stirred and slowly focused on her face.

"I want to visit them."

"Who?"

"Jeffrey."

"He called?"

"No."

"Oh."

"We've got the address."

"We do. But have we been invited?"

"No."

The worry on her face since their son had married that girl, worse than the bickering he'd predicted years ago, the behind the back moaning he'd envisaged if Jeffrey lived down the road with a wife and brought up children differently to how they'd raised him. Such griping would be welcome now.

"When do you want to go?"

"Saturday."

"Alright then. Saturday it is."

His genial agreement made Jane worry more. He must think there was a problem too.

"Miriam wants to come."

"I'm not sure that's a good idea."

"Why not?"

"Don't get defensive."

"I'm just asking why."

"Never mind. Forget it."

~

The outside of the apartment block was bright and white, not what they'd expected at all. It was like a photograph from a modern design magazine. How could their son afford it?

"It looks nice."

"Lovely."

"Hmm..." said Jane. The vase she'd bought was wrapped in silver paper, cold and neutral.

"What number is it?" asked John.

"3A."

The buzzer for 3A didn't have a name next to it. 3B was Maryville, 1A Sharood. All the buzzers except 3A and 1B were accounted for.

"Are you sure? It could be 1B."

"He said they have a good view," was snapped in reply.

Miriam stopped their bickering by pushing the button. The intercom crackled.

"Yes?"

"Susan?" There was no answer. "Susan, is that you? Hello?"

"Who is this?"

Jane grasped hold of Miriam's arm.

"It's Jane, Jeffrey's mother. And John."

"And Miriam. Hi Susan," she called cheerfully.

Six eyes fluttered madly, trying to think of what to do next.

"Susan," said John. "Are you there?"

"I'll come down."

"Odd," mouthed Miriam.

They waited patiently. Jane's gut told her something was very wrong.

"I've got a bad feeling."

"No," said Miriam. "Don't you dare let her see you cry."

Jane pinched the bridge of her nose, wiped her fingers over the smudged eyeliner and took a deep breath.

"Should we buzz again?" asked Miriam.

"Give her a chance," said John, tutting as he raised his eyebrows.

He'd always been polite to Susan, knew what it was like to marry into a family of strong minded women, but in the months since the wedding he'd begun to see his wife's point of view. His daughter-in-law had been particularly unwelcoming. Jane going on about it got on his nerves but to not call, that wasn't like Jeffrey. He'd only behave like that if someone told him to. John knew his son was weak minded, easily led, too molly coddled, that's what John's mother used to say. But damn it, he was their only child and they'd waited and wanted for nineteen years before he came along. When their hope had gone and all his wife's tears had been cried, they were told her suspected older lady symptoms were actually a baby.

They were an isolated unit. At thirty nine Jane had

found the other mothers too young and full of nonsense. She didn't like their clothes, their decor, their let them cry it outs and haven't you got it easy only having one? 'You've no idea,' she'd think. All those years, all that pain to get to that point. Jeffrey was in the crook of her arms from the day he was born and hooked on her hip from the week he could hold himself up. Jane was deliriously happy spending days at home with her darling boy. He was taught please and thank you, got nothing if he stomped his feet, but was he too adored? Was he made so secure he thought nothing bad could happen to him so he didn't see Susan coming, didn't know the damage to your life a disturbed person could do?

The door to the apartment block opened. She looked no different. Miriam had hoped her face would have softened, the old anger dissipated in some way.

"We've come to see Jeffrey. And you. The happy couple in their new home."

Jane held out the gift. Susan pushed the key to the apartment into the lock, keeping her heel against the door.

"I'm afraid I have some bad news."

A fury rose in John, a need to protect his child combined with the realisation that he was too late.

"Jeffrey had an accident."

John put his hands around Susan's neck. She didn't try to defend herself even when the back of her head was cracked hard against the wall three times. Miriam pulled him off her. He ran his knuckles over the bricks then his elbows then his cheeks, needing to purge his guilt with immediate physical pain.

"I'm sorry," he wailed to his wife. "I didn't listen."

Jane had fallen to her knees. "No," was all she said.

She had a baby in her arms, moved him to her hip, now he was by her side. She cocooned herself in his love and blanked the outside world.

Miriam was glad she'd come for such different reasons to those she'd imagined.

"What happened?" she asked.

"He was drunk and drove into the river. He drowned."

"By accident?"

"What?"

Miriam knew Jeffrey drank too much. She'd seen him put empty spirit bottles from his car into a public bin. She'd had a subtle word with him about people who drink and drive, people who drink too much, too often. Too subtle.

"When? Why didn't you tell us? When's the funeral?" She saw a flicker of fear on Susan's face. "My god. Tell me he's not buried already."

Jane looked up at her younger sister. Miriam shoved Susan.

"You reeled him right in," shouted John. "Our son. We'll call the police on you."

Susan put her hands behind her back and turned the key in the lock.

"They already know about it. Who do you think told me?"

"You're not right in the head, you know that?"

Susan's vision was blurred from the bumps and the pain was intensifying. She opened the door. Jane grabbed her ankle. Susan tried to shake her off.

"Was he in pain? Would it have hurt? Do you think he knew what was happening?" Little toddler boy running into her arms, big wet kiss on her cheek. "I love you more than anything," she'd say. "More than ice cream?" he'd laugh. "Oh you're right, maybe not as much as that," she'd joke back.

Susan wanted to kick her mother-in-law away. She shook her leg, trying not to warrant an assault charge.

"They said he wouldn't have felt a thing. He banged his head. He was unconscious so wouldn't have known what was happening."

Jane let go and Susan locked herself behind the glass door of the apartment block. They all stared at her, confused. She'd rather they'd attacked the door, screamed at her, tried to hurt her more.

"It was an accident. I wasn't even there."

She stumbled up the communal stairway and knelt in front of the living room window. Her visitors slowly helped each other into a brown saloon car. Miriam drove. Jane and John were curled up on the back seat. Susan digested the scene. Aunt Miriam was likely to cause trouble and the dad had been stronger than she'd expected. She felt the back of her head where it hurt, warm blood coated her fingertips. She'd better call her solicitor.

"Mr Carew. It's Mrs Jeffreys. I'll sell for eight thousand seven hundred."

"Excuse me?"

"If we complete and transfer by next Friday."

"That's impossible."

"If you can't, I'll find someone who can. You know it's a bargain."

He hoped her acidity didn't remain in the apartment when she was gone.

"Leave it with me."

"We have a deal then?"

"Yes. Now if you'll excuse me, I've got a lot to organise."

He hung up, excitement rising. Thirty five per cent less than its market value. He'd pay the deposit, his sister the mortgage, any future profits equally split. Perfect.

Susan felt nauseous so lay on the sofa and was asleep within minutes. When she woke up she was too dizzy to stay upright so took herself to hospital, just in case, because heads could be tricky things: the jaw, the brain, the matter, the pain, the hurt, the feelings, the lack of a feeling.

~

A doctor sat on the edge of the bed. Susan hated the invasion of her space but was too weak to push him off. She would have to find another way to derail him. He pushed his glasses higher up his nose and shook his head pityingly as he turned to look at her.

"I see you were a nurse so I'll get straight to the point Mrs Jeffreys." Still a nurse she thought, still able. "When you fell unconscious for a second time we scanned your head. The wound is fixable but there's internal damage and I'm afraid your sense of smell may be affected." When she didn't react he carried on. "We found an older set of scars. Have you fallen before Mrs Jeffreys? Or had a hurt placed upon you?"

"No."

"There'd be no shame in it."

"No."

"Can you taste your food?"

"No."

"That's very tough. Life must have been very hard."

"Nope."

"As I said, I'm afraid the new injury is likely to mean

your sense of smell will be affected, by how much we're not sure..."

He shrugged: could be this, could be that, could be the other.

She shrugged: water off a duck's back, who cares, doesn't bother me. Don't be nice, don't dare be nice and make me cry, god-damn you.

"Susan, we tend to find that those who have lost such senses, the two of them together, they often feel a terrible sense of isolation. They miss what others take for granted, are unable to understand what it is to feel. And they get angry. Furious moods can visit them when the sense of smell and flavour are gone. We're not sure why. Family members say it's like they aren't the same person anymore."

She squeezed her eyes together, nothing would dribble from their edges.

"Can you fetch the nurse? I need to piss."

"I'm here to help you Susan. We all are."

"In that case you can hold the bedpan beneath me." She glared at his pity. "The pain is intense this evening. Can you tell the nurse I need the strongest painkillers. And tomorrow when I'm discharged, what will help me most is you writing a decent prescription."

~

John Jeffreys drove to Susan and Jeffrey's apartment armed with notes from his solicitor and confirmation from the police that nothing untoward had happened to his son. It helped a little to think Susan hadn't literally pushed him into the water. It hurt a lot to think she'd made him so miserable and they hadn't known. The police found three empty bottles of whiskey in his car plus two empty wine bottles and numerous finished beer bottles in a cool box in the boot. The only reason to drink that much was to hide pain, surely.

"Not a happy man," said the officer.

"But to drive into the water?" asked John.

"A mistake, I'm sure. The bends on that road are treacherous."

They phoned the coroner's office to double check the injuries. The young man told them there was nothing on the file but drowning and a bump to the head from where he'd cracked it against the windscreen. No stab wound to the heart or bruises around the throat. They spoke to their doctor, their local police officer, their priest and a pathologist who'd recently joined the congregation. All of them felt for the Jeffreys, right in their core, but none had an answer that could lay the blame on anyone else. It was simply a tragedy.

"It was her," said John.

"That's not what they say," Jane replied.

"She drove him to it, had something to do with it, I'm sure she did."

Jane started to cry. He left the room, unable to deal with the fact that he'd ignored all his wife's worries and encouraged the marriage thinking it would make Jeffrey grow up and take some responsibility for his life.

~

John stepped in front of a man holding a blue plastic crate. A pile of boxes stood in the foyer, taller than the cacti guarding the stairs. There was green carpet on the floor, thick, luxurious, expensive, too good for shoes. Did Jeffrey have an insurance policy? Did Susan push him over the edge for that? John would have given her the money if that's what she was after. No need for her to ask twice if it had meant she'd be willing to disappear on them.

He climbed the stairs and looped around two corners. There was apartment 3A, its door half open. Music muffled voices. Was she in there with a new beau, laughing at them? He touched the silver 3A lettering with his fingertips to make sure he was in the right place then entered the apartment and walked down the hallway.

"Susan?"

The talking stopped.

"Can I help you?" Mr Carew appeared behind John. The old man looked confused, tired. Scabs were healing on his arms and face as if he'd recently fallen. "Sir?"

A lady with jet black hair in a bob appeared in front of them.

"Is Susan here?" John asked. "I'm looking for Susan."

"There's no Susan here I'm afraid," replied the lady. "Maybe she's in another apartment? This is 3A. There was a lady in 2B who said hello. She seemed nice. Could that be her?"

"No. Susan Jeffreys, apartment 3A. She lives right here."

He pointed at the floor.

"That's who we bought it from." The man put the box down and held out his hand. John automatically shook it. "I'm Sidney Carew and this is my sister Charlotte."

"John Jeffreys."

"Oh," Charlotte's hand moved to her heart as if it had suddenly skipped a beat. "I'm so sorry for your loss."

John's eyes hardened. "When did she move out?"

"Yesterday."

"Thursday," Charlotte corrected. "I wanted to have the table delivered midday on Friday but she said she'd be gone by then so I had to re-arrange for today and... Are you alright?"

Sidney caught John's weight by the elbows and led him to a chair.

"Would you like some water? I'll try and find a glass."

"I didn't think you could sell a place so fast."

"You'd be surprised," said Sidney. "Where there's a will, there's a... I mean. She had a lot of the paperwork prepared already."

"You're awfully pale. Shall I call a doctor?" Charlotte didn't want a strange old man dying in her kitchen, haunting her new home.

"It took months to buy our house. I thought this'd be the same."

John sipped the tepid water.

"It was all in her name, ready to go as soon as the price was agreed."

Sidney had arranged a bridging loan so they didn't lose it. He couldn't arrange a mortgage that fast for his once in a lifetime bargain. Charlotte had wanted to live in the area for so long, had thought she'd never be able to afford it. Now she'd cheer up. Finally, she'd move on.

"Did she leave a forwarding address?"

They both shook their heads.

"A PO Box?"

"No."

"Nothing? Who's her solicitor?" John asked. "Well?"

Charlotte looked fearful. This wasn't how it was meant to be. John saw them exchange a glance.

"I am," said Sidney.

"It was all legal, all agreed, wasn't it Sid?"

"She was a strange one," her brother replied.

John stepped round the box in the hallway.

"I really am so sorry for your loss," Charlotte called after him.

"You enjoy your gain," John raged back.

He'd thought he couldn't feel more angry but knowing that others had profited from Jeffrey's death, he hadn't prepared himself for that. Humans could be so selfish. The car engine hid their calls. Two ladies and the man banged on the windows and the car bonnet.

"She left this. She left this."

He wound down the window.

"I'm Lola from 2B. Thank goodness I saw them. She left this for you, said you'd be coming."

It was a cardboard box, light from the way she was carrying it, the size of forty eight cans of tomatoes. There was a white envelope taped to the top. John turned the engine off and opened the boot, putting it next to his puncture kit.

~

Jane hurried down the hallway when she heard the key in the lock, thinking her son was home.

"You were out? I didn't notice."

John put the box in the cupboard under the stairs. He'd opened it in the car. Jeffrey's watch and his briefcase, the one they'd bought him as a congratulations on getting his first job. A silver tankard. A black photo frame containing a picture of the three of them. That hurt. And a note. Details of where the body was stored and written authorisation from Mrs Susan Jeffreys that would allow Mr and Mrs Jeffreys to bury their only son.

"Were you gone a long time?"

"Not really."

"Good."

He'd declined the offer of pills for himself but understood why she took them. Anything to make you forget, to dull the maddening agony.

"I went for a walk," he said. "Did you eat?"

"What?"

"Did you eat?"

"I'm not hungry."

"No. Me neither."

"It's all wrong you know."

"I know."

He took her hands. He hugged her.

The Labour

Susan moved further West to a town John and Jane had never mentioned, where the morgue boy wouldn't see her bump grow so he wouldn't run away from what she needed him for. She twitched, plotted and ate chocolate ice cream as she worked out how to create a better future.

~

At the maternity clinic Susan stood next to the pale blue wall. She didn't lean. She wasn't huge like the two ladies who were sitting down.

One of them flicked through a magazine. The other started a conversation but changed the focus when only a couple of sentences in. The chattering failed to conceal her fear of giving birth and motherhood. Susan was glad the babbler hadn't tried talking to her. She'd have got short shrift and was no doubt one of those emotional ones who burst into tears at a harsh look let alone a curt word.

The size of their bellies appalled Susan. She'd never taken notice of pregnant ladies waddling to maternity wards but now she was expecting it was hard not to stare. The littlest one was how Susan had morosely pictured herself when full term. The largest was beyond what she'd imagined, like a ripe melon about to burst. As Susan watched, the lady rubbed her hand over and around her belly then bent down to kiss it but her reach was three inches too far away so she puckered her lips at the air instead. Disturbed by the natural affection, Susan looked at the floor. She felt a familiar wave of nausea so left the room. She'd racked her brains to think of an anti-sickness medicine she could take that wouldn't harm the baby. She'd have risked taking one that might damage it if it weren't for the fact that she'd be the one who had to care for it. Life would be hard enough without some mental or physical defect thrown in.

Back in the waiting room, the chatterer was on her own.

"The sickness goes. It's more uncomfortable now but at least that sickness has gone."

She smiled expectantly, waiting for Susan to ask her how long she had to go.

"I know. I'm a nurse. It's the hard part for you now though. Let's hope you both get through it. My sister's baby died."

The lady gasped. Susan picked up a magazine full of advertisements for prams, cots, bedding, things she wouldn't buy until the very end as there was no point spending money when it might all go wrong. She'd heard stories, seen midwives with new born ghosts reflected in their eyes, weeping once they were away from the devastated nearly parents.

As she moved to a seat the gusset of her tights pulled up in a way that made her groan, reminding her of the morgue boy.

"Are you alright?"

"Miss Smith," a midwife called.

Using her hands for leverage Miss Smith rose and Susan spotted the fingers on her left hand were bare. A second midwife appeared.

"Mrs Jeffreys."

Susan followed the click clacking of keys and pens that hung round her neck, over the navy uniform.

"So, how are you feeling?"

"Fine," she said. No need to shout, she thought.

"Good, good."

The midwife plonked a blue cardboard folder on the desk. It was ripped at one corner even though this was only Susan's second visit.

"Soooooo, you're feeling good?"

"Yes."

She felt pudgy.

"Wonderful. You look well, you're feeling well?" Susan couldn't place the accent. "Let's weigh you. Shoes off and pop yourself onto the scales. Wow, 4lbs more than last time, it's going to be a big baby. Any worries, concerns? You look well. No problems eh? All strong and healthy."

Susan could squash the midwife's enthusiasm flat with my husband died, I had sex with a stranger from the morgue, is that bad?

"All fine."

Her blood pressure was checked, tummy squashed, finger pricked for a few drops of blood.

"Now then…" The keys around the midwife's neck jangled constantly. One of them had a pink teddy bear hanging from it. How could she bear the constant fuss? It would drive Susan mad. "Your next appointment is in four weeks then four weeks again, then seven after that. Exciting huh?"

"I have to go."

"Of course, getting your hair done?"

"What? No. Why would you say that?"

The midwife smiled as she shrugged. Her jaunty jangling followed Susan down the corridor.

"Mrs Alsom," was called. A pretty girl with jet black curls beamed at the midwife. No doubt she would be a natural.

~

"You've a while to go yet."

The groaning persisted for another fourteen hours.

"You've not dilated much, only two centimetres more than last night, that's a total of four."

"Damn it all to hell and back."

Susan admonished the whole world. Her husband was lucky to be dead. If he were alive she'd raid the cupboards for a scalpel and slice him.

~

Finally.

"Okay. Here we go Mrs Jeffreys. Push!"

"I'm going to rip open and die," she screamed.

The baby tore her apart. The pain of the contractions though intense and exhausting was nothing compared to the burning, searing agony of the baby fighting free of her womb. And it didn't stop. The midwife had said *it will end*. Turned out she was a liar.

"It still hurts."

"The contractions keep going for a bit. It's good. It means the placenta's coming out."

Nurse Benson put a bowl under her patient, to catch the placenta and check it was all there.

"We've got a breech."

She pulled a red cord. A bell buzzed. Susan didn't understand. One of the midwives had the baby in her arms and was clearing the mucus from its airways.

"You've got a beautiful baby girl. One second then you can hold her."

"Okay Susan, you're doing really well," added the other midwife.

"Don't patronise me," she screamed as a contraction pushed her further apart. Blood seeped over the table, crept menacingly towards the edges of the sheet. "What's happening?"

"You're having twins," the midwife said brightly, as though Susan was finding out in her first doctor's appointment and it was the happiest news in the world.

"No. Stitch me up!"

A contraction seized her. She mooed like a crazed cow. A man in a mask walked purposely into the room.

"Mrs Jeffreys, let's see how you're doing."

His tone was too cheerful. Susan never spoke to patients in such a ridiculously happy way. If she weren't bleeding so much, wasn't so tired, in so much pain, she'd retort, "how do you think you fool." But nurses mustn't speak to doctors that way. She'd lose her job. Some patients had already asked that she wasn't assigned to them again. Fine. The ones that were really poorly were too ill to care, were so close to death that they appreciated her getting straight to any point because they didn't have time for messing.

"Too late for a C section, too hard to push it back. It's a stubborn little fella."

"A boy? There you go. One of each. How lovely," cooed the midwife.

"A figure of speech. Not necessarily male. Soon have you sorted Mrs Jeffreys. Suck on that gas now, ready for a slight pulling sensation."

Dr James's gloved hands slipped in the blood. "Woah there."

The gap was wide from the ripping, easy if it weren't for her haemorrhaging. He nodded to the midwife to stand by. The patient looked like a little girl, scrap of a thing, probably a druggie. He pulled the baby by the bum, trying not to dislocate its fragile hips. Susan's scream shot through the ward, the windows, across apartments, bars and shops. Eleven people at the hospital bus stop shuddered.

"It's a female," the doctor announced.

The baby was quiet. Susan hoped it was dead, she hadn't been expecting it anyway. How dare it cause her such pain? How dare the both of them? Instinct told her to roll to the side, clutch her belly, fall asleep and wake up when they were all gone but her legs were stuck in stirrups as they laboriously stitched her up.

"You have two beautiful girls."

There was a midwife on either side of her, a baby in each of their arms, one noticeably smaller than the other.

"Would you like to hold them?"

"No."

"How about they latch on, have a snuggle with their mummy?"

"No." Susan shut her eyes. "Why is that one so small?"

"I guess she got less food in the womb. It happens. She's beautiful though, alert for a new born. She's a bright little princess, don't you think Doris?"

"Absolutely. Definitely. This one's asleep, bless her."

Doris chuckled and beamed, willing Mrs Jeffreys to

open her eyes, get involved.

"Runt."

"Pardon?"

"She's the runt of the litter."

The midwives had both seen mothers who were sad, nearly died, angry at what they'd been put through, but those words, never before. Doris had one of her doom and gloom feelings and wished, not for the first time, that she could take the babies home and save them from a life of pain. As if sensing her worry, the baby started to cry.

"Okay darling. Someone's hungry. Why don't you have a little go?"

Susan agreed for medical reasons: to force her womb to contract, to empty her heavy bosoms, to stop infections setting in. Doris's smile faltered. A parent always stroked the head and said you're so beautiful, I love you my little angel, or some such phrase. Mrs Jeffreys was feeding the baby but staring at the wall. No caring, no kissing, no nothing.

"You're doing so well. How about the other one?"

The happiness Doris felt at the successful birth disappeared. She'd have a word with the ward sister, mark the chart so Mrs Jeffreys would be checked thoroughly before being discharged.

"Wonderful. That's fantastic. You must have done this before?" Silence. "Shall we call in your husband?"

~

In the ward Susan slept through the crying. Nurse Freda woke her.

"Here you go. Here's baby…" There was no first name on the tag on her ankle. "I heard about the surprise. Guess you had one name and now need two that go together."

The baby's mouth opened and closed, searching for more milk.

"That's all you're getting," Susan told it. "As you've decided to be a twin you can learn to do with less. Pass me the other one."

The first baby that had been fed now cried.

"Hey little one," said Nurse Freda. "What's the matter?"

"Leave her," Susan snapped.

"It's alright. I can cuddle her. I'd love to."

"I said leave her. She has to get used to being left. I've only one pair of hands. They can both get used to waiting."

The nurses were trained to do as the mother asked. Each woman had her own way of coping and staff weren't meant to interfere but Nurse Freda hated hearing a baby cry. She had to grab the cot rail to stop herself from picking it up and snuggling.

The Revelation

Susan was filled with immense sadness as she stared at the white sheet her legs were resting on, a blood stain as big as her hand visible beside her right hip. The nurse hadn't noticed it and Susan hadn't asked for the sheets to be changed. They were busy. She could live with a little blood. She'd lost two litres after the birth so what was a spot on a sheet, drying out, turning maroon already.

She'd never felt such terrible melancholy before. She could cry. And she never cried, not in front of people, never since that day, waking up that night, the ability to taste gone from her. But five days after giving birth to two daughters she was overwhelmed. Her head drooped, too dense for her neck muscles to hold it upright. Her lungs were working hard to capture air beneath her heavy shoulders, breasts full of milk that leaked onto her nightie. Sore. No-one had said how tender they would be. Her brain felt desolate, abandoned, confused about the pointlessness of humans, of life, the desperately unhappy emotions it was sending into her heart, making it beat slowly as if unsure about whether it wanted to keep going or not.

A baby cried. The damp stain on the right hand side of her nightie widened. Susan didn't look to see which child was wailing. She couldn't tell the difference between their sounds yet and wasn't sure she wanted to be able to identify them. It wasn't fair that because she was the one to carry them and give birth to them, she had to look after them. Why must it be her? There were two fathers, she was sure of that, and both fathers had abandoned her. She could feel it in her gut that the littlest was the morgue boy's and the bigger one Jeffrey's but who would believe her. She wept, quietly so no-one noticed, smearing the tears across her cheeks with the skin on her wrists as she didn't have a tissue. Her upper body juddered. Now she'd started she couldn't stop.

The crying baby was the one nearest her with its legs clenched into its stomach, face scrunched up like an ugly wrinkly creature. Susan didn't want to pick it up. She didn't care for it or the other one, not at that moment. A nurse she hadn't seen before appeared beside the cots.

"Hey little darlings. Which is it this time? Why it's number one. Come here my beauty. Let's pass you to your mama."

Susan didn't want to be someone's mama. She wanted to sleep so she turned her back on the nurse and the baby. The nurse walked round to the wall Susan was facing.

"Here you go Susan. I know you're tired but how about a feed for your eldest then I'll pop her back in the cot and you can have a snooze."

Susan scowled at the nurse's tummy that was level with her head. There was a stain on her uniform. Scrappy. Unprofessional. Susan would have changed rather than have excretions on show to patients. There must be a slack Sister on duty because she shouldn't have let that pass. Susan closed her eyes. The crying didn't go away. When she opened them, the nurse was walking up and down by the side of the bed, rocking the baby in her arms, smiling and being all hello little lovely hungry are we.

"Take her."

"Sorry?"

"You can have her. Take her home with you. I don't want her. I've had enough. And the other one, the both of them. God-damn bastard babies."

Susan knew the words were bad as she said them but she couldn't help herself. The nurse checked the baby's wrist band.

"Day five," she declared. "Your milk's coming in. I knew it. That's why you're feeling out of sorts. I bet you feel like bursting into tears don't you? It's perfectly normal you know, always on day five. No-one knows why but I can promise you it always, always happens. Day five is the worst one. Don't you worry sweetie. I promise it'll get better, really it will."

Susan wasn't sure how with no husband at home to fetch her things or bring her bread and water. She couldn't stop the tears from falling even though she tried her hardest. She cried as the nurse latched the baby onto her breast and head back, eyes to the ceiling, she wept, wondering what her life had become. Two babies were not what she'd planned for. One was meant to be all she bothered with. She allowed herself a peep at the baby's face to see if she loved it but when she watched it sucking, as she started to feel the life force being pulled out of her, she begrudged the child for the energy it took, energy she needed in order to heal so she could piss like a normal person, not be in pain, be able to walk again.

When the nurse patted her arm Susan imagined resting

her head in the crook of her shoulder, accepting a hug and some there there comfort. She hated herself for that because it was not her. What had the babies done, five days into her life and they'd already turned her into someone she didn't recognise. How dare they? She was strong, didn't take to fools, didn't appreciate weakness, wouldn't stand for it. She couldn't survive being a wuss. That was not her, anger was. If she became a weeping minnow her life would be pathetic and her children needy. She had to buckle up, raise them to be resilient like she was because it was a shitty world and being all oh woe is me was no good for anyone. The wall started to rise as her cheeks dried. She stopped crying, pursed her lips. Look at that bastardly morgue boy, running down the street like a childish coward. She would find him now she'd given birth and she would tell him the babies were his and he would have to help her.

~

Susan accepted all the medication the hospital offered. There was no point being sore, it was best to keep on top of the pain. Her hormones fluctuated so much she missed her husband, felt like punching the boy, turned momentarily crazy at what she had become and hoped, pushing her mouth into the pillow when the lights were out, that she'd fall asleep and never wake up again. They offered her a tub of pills on the day she was discharged, for the wounds, for the fifty three stitches, to numb the throbbing and halt the infection.

"You're going home today?" a junior doctor asked. He'd watched the tail end of the birth thinking the stitches being sewn through her by his mentor were too tight. "Those stitches, are they sore? We can loosen them."

"They're fine." It hurt to walk, to sit, to lift the babies, to shit, to piss, to everything.

"Who's collecting you?"

"A taxi."

"Excellent. You be careful with those stitches now, there's a lot of them. Have you got plenty of help at home?"

"I know what I'm doing."

"Of course you do." He patted her hand. She swatted him away. "Mrs Jeffreys, I hope you don't mind me saying but something's been puzzling me. The placenta, the midwife was worried it had broken, more than one bit in the bowl and all that so I checked it carefully as one should and it looked like two placentas to me, really, definitely two placentas. I can see why the midwife thought otherwise because one was much smaller but they were both whole so I kept them and—"

"You kept them?"

"Yes, you see it's rare but..." He sat on the edge of the bed. Susan cringed, moving her legs away from his hip. "There's such a thing as superfetation, when two foetus's share a womb having been conceived at different times. And with one of your girls being so much smaller. Do you think? Is it possible?"

Jeffrey and the morgue boy: two fathers, two babies, one mother, one birth day, the watch, the sofa, the stain from what had escaped her insides. She knew she'd felt different afterwards, more nauseous, breasts even sorer, belly fuller. And the doctor was thinking what she'd thought. Right again, Susan.

"Of course it's unusual, incredibly rare. I ran some tests and—"

"I don't think so."

It was the perfect subject for his thesis. No-one else would be covering it. He'd get his first paper published and his career was bound to flourish afterwards. The doctor had expected Mrs Jeffreys to want to know everything she could. He pulled a sheet of paper from his file.

"I copied this for you. It tells you more about it. Really it's quite wonderful, amazing what the female body can do. Your husband might—"

"I have no husband."

"Oh."

"I'm a widow."

"I'm so sorry. I—"

"I've enough to deal with. I won't allow you to use me."

She dismissed him with a flick of her chin and he hurried away before she got him in trouble. He kicked the wall in the gents.

"Shit. Shit. Shit. Shit. Shit."

Seven weeks until the deadline and he hadn't started writing his paper yet. He returned to the ward, picked a trainee nurse.

"Nurse Jennings, beautiful Nurse Jennings, I hope you're going to the dance on Friday," he winked. "Do you happen to have the notes for bed nine?"

"That pile."

He flicked to the back of the file, all the way to Susan's first appointment. Her status had changed from married to widowed seven weeks in, one square scribbled out, a big star by the married tick box. Which explained her reaction. Naughty Mrs Jeffreys hadn't grieved for very long.

~

Nurse Aldridge left the ward to check if Susan's taxi had arrived. She pitied the poor lady with two babies, no-one to drive the three of them home.

Susan muttered like she used to when she was a child so the bad feelings got out but no-one could hear them.

"Why should you get to die and you get to run off? How come you get to go off and do something different whereas me, I'm left with one in each arm, not even a hand free for myself. Imagine the shame if I dumped them in an orphanage. The staff would look at me with pity assuming I wasn't able to cope, not understanding that I'm leaving them there because I hate them. I can cope. Of course I can. How dare anyone think I can't. I won't be beaten by these two or you two, you two that left me. Two against one. It's always two against me isn't it. Him and her, and her and her, they were against me growing up and now this lot. Well I won't back away. I'll win without taking pleasure in it. Some things you only do to know you're done so you can tick them off a list: task at work, finished, tick, done, essay for nursing, finished, tick, done, raising two children, finished, tick when done, eighteen and they're out, no longer my responsibility, nothing to do with me. I could leave them down an alley and not look back or see me saying to a woman on a beach would you mind looking after my little ones while I go to the bathroom. Of course not, she'll say. They're adorable. I'll slip away and get on the bus that's just pulled in, then another bus and another and then I wouldn't be trapped looking after them except they'd find me wouldn't they? The police would print out posters saying red hat, brown dress, brown sandals. I'd be caught and vilified. So what else is there? There's only the one thing but it's dangerous.

What if I left marks? And I was trained to save lives not take them though they ripped my lower regions apart, hurt deep inside of me and cry when there's nothing wrong. Shut up you shit-faced little fuckers."

Baby one stopped crying. She took in a deep gulp of air which she then burped out and as if sensing her sister's fright, the other one also went silent.

"Taxi's here," said Nurse Aldridge, poking her head round the curtain.

Susan grinned as she imagined herself a film star in one of those movies set in the Southern states of America.

"Wonderful. Aren't they just divine? Don't you just adore them?"

~

On the ride back to her rented apartment Susan knew her experiment had failed. She felt nothing towards the babies on either side of her which meant she was like her mother. It was in the genes, had to be. She hadn't felt anything positive since the knock to the head aged nine and the babies hadn't awakened an ability to care. She would remain alone whilst living with them, isolated from the normality of the world which she didn't understand.

Her stomach rumbled after her refusal of toast at the hospital that morning but what was the point of eating. It gurgled loudly, desperate for sustenance for the feeding. She remembered. She remembered the rumbling. And her stupid, foolish, immature inability to ignore a need for food even though she could sense the tension emanating from her mother's body as it lay on the sofa with a damp and dirty, what was meant to be white facecloth over her eyes. Her father and sister were out. Stupid foolish Susan.

"What time's dinner please?"

"You had your lunch at school," her mother snapped, pressing her lips together tightly. She raised her left hand to the cloth, pushing it more firmly onto her forehead. "Jesus. I never get a moment's peace in this world."

"Sorry. Don't worry. I'm not hungry."

"No. If I have to cook the precious princess's bloody dinner I'd better get up, never mind my bloody migraine."

"I don't want any."

"Don't lie."

"I'm not. I—"

"Shut up."

Susan flattened herself against the wall as her mother pushed past her to the kitchen, then ran up the stairs, wishing she hadn't disturbed her. She sat on the edge of her bed waiting to be called down to eat. The noise of the pans being banged around got louder. Susan cringed. She shouldn't have asked about food, not when her mother was having one of *those* days. Susan was old enough to know better, old enough to ask for permission to make her own sandwich and offer her mother one too. That's what a reasonable child would have done. She did not feel reasonable. She picked teddy off the bed and hugged him close. He smelt of soap from the sheets. She kissed his head and rocked from side to side as she squeezed him. The bell being rung made her jump. She ran. She must not be slow to the table, not after the fuss she'd created. She must be worthy and appreciative.

Her mother was already at the top of the stairs.

"I called out dinner while I was setting the table. Dinner I shouted as I drained the potatoes. Why didn't you come after I'd called out dinner? I rang the bell and when I didn't hear your footsteps straight away I ran here. You made me run you little tyke. Dinner's ready. Why didn't you come? You're SO rude. Come down NOW."

Woe betide Susan if she didn't hurry in front of her mother down the stairs, terrified of a shove that would send her flying, expecting to be picked up by the scruff of the neck and flung across the room. Susan slunk in front of the table and sat on her usual chair. Her mother put a plate in front of her.

"Thank you," her mother said.

"Thank you," Susan repeated.

"Say it nicely."

"Thank you." Her lips trembled, pathetic child.

Her mother drank some water and sat there, watching her daughter.

"Eat."

Susan's eyes looked to the ceiling.

"Eat it."

She stared back down at the plate full of cauliflower, potatoes, and chicken that had been boiled rather than fried meaning there was a pink tinge surrounding it and a string of fat hanging off a bloodied cyst. Pools of water gathered where the vegetables hadn't been drained properly.

"Don't make me make you eat it."

"I had chicken at school."

"So?"

Susan picked her fork up and stuck it in a floret of cauliflower that promptly fell apart. She scooped the slithers onto her fork but didn't lift the food to her mouth.

"Is there any gravy?"

"No. Eat what you're given and be thankful."

Susan knew she should eat, people were starving, orphans lived on the streets in India.

"Eat it."

She raised the fork to her mouth but the smell made her gag. She rested it on the plate again.

"Eat."

"I can't."

"Eat it."

Her mother jumped up to Susan's side of the table quicker than she could run away. Arm around one shoulder, holding her in place, she grabbed a chunk of potato with her fingers and tried to shove it in her daughter's mouth. Susan leant her head back, trying to escape. Her eyes looked at the wall, away from her mother.

"Eat it. Eat it. Eat your stupid dinner."

Susan's lips were clamped shut. Her mother tried to get her fingers between them. She hurt the child by leaning all her adult weight on Susan's thigh, making her cry in pain so that her mouth opened and in went some food. Susan tried to spit it out. Her mother held her chin up so she couldn't open her mouth to get rid of it.

"Eat your dinner."

She grabbed the fork, scooped up the chicken and pressed it onto Susan's lips. The metal pushed down on her skin. Susan opened her mouth a centimetre and the fork banged against her teeth as her mother forced the meat into her. "Argh," she cried as the prong scraped the roof of her mouth. Tears cascaded down her cheeks. She gagged and sobbed as she chewed. Her mother shoved in another mouthful. And another.

"I spent my time cooking that so you can bloody well eat it all."

When the plate was halfway empty Susan's mother saw herself from the outside looking in, a big girl pressing on a little girl, her head locked in her arm. She let go and stood back.

"Go and wash your face. No snacks later. You can go hungry, not eating the food I took time out of my afternoon to cook for you when I didn't even want to. You're the one who asked for it. It wasn't my idea."

Before Susan could make it to the door she was sick over the parquet flooring, coming to a halt in the middle of her pool of vomit, chicken bits under her toes, bile as their gravy. She retched again and leant back so the sick cascaded down her front rather than over the floor and knew she'd made a mistake as that meant two things needed washing - her clothes and the wood. She should have stuck with staining one thing, to make life easier, her punishment simpler. She stayed staring at the door as her mother stared at her. It was so close but she couldn't move to reach it and where would she go? No room had a lock, not after last time when she'd made it to the bathroom and turned the key to protect herself. Best thing would be for her to stay and accept whatever punishment she was given then start life again tomorrow. Pain was only temporary, it came and went until the next time.

She heard her mother moving but still distant. She tipped her head down and slightly to the right where she glimpsed her mother clearing the table, wiping food from the floor, kicking her bare foot against the skirting board so hard it made her bend over in pain. After a minute she tried wiggling her toes. The littlest two really hurt. Look at what her daughter had done, hurting the mother. And there it was. She flew, raging, grabbed the child from the back, swung her round not caring what she hit, kept on swinging until she let go with an aim at the fireplace and with a crack that was that. The child was on the floor, asleep, no longer harming her.

As Susan slept her mother washed the floor then she curled up on the sofa in the front room. When she woke, her husband was kneeling beside her.

"Was she naughty?"

"I don't remember."

"We'll have to call a doctor."

"I don't need one. Just fetch me a pill, a blue one. I've a terrible headache."

Her husband sat back on his haunches. Such a shame after such a lovely day with little Alice. If they'd only had her as a child then life would be so much more manage-able. He took the smelling salts from the cupboard in the kitchen and waved them under his eldest daughter's nose. After the fourth minute she stirred, opening her eyes but giving him nothing.

"You fell and banged your head, all better now so that's lucky."

Susan didn't feel lucky.

He carried her to bed and she slept on her side as the back of her head hurt too much to put weight on it. In the morning her father brought her a glass of apple juice as a treat. She took a sip. Although it was thicker than water there was no flavour. She sipped again and it was the same again. She fell asleep for too long. Her mother com-plained at the cost of the visiting doctor. On the third day after the accident when she ate a piece of toast coated in strawberry jam, it may as well have been a warm piece of cardboard.

"I can't taste anything."

"What are you talking about?"

"The jam, it's got no flavour or the butter or the bread."

"Mine's fine," said Alice.

"Always so silly Susan," said her mother. "Go away. Go to your room. Now. You're annoying me."

Sitting on her bed, Susan grabbed her teddy. She punched him twice in the face then threw him on the floor and stamped on his torso so hard that a seam split and white cotton oozed out of his cuts. She hated his weakness, him lying there like a helpless idiot. She had no time for idiots, people like her sister who hesitated before answering questions, wanting to please the adults. Susan would go to Alice's room later and pinch her to show the displeasure she felt at being related to such a creature. She kicked the teddy across the room then stared at the trail of its innards. Nothing. She no longer felt any love for it, no yearning to hug it and rub her cheek against his soft fur. In fact, never mind love, truth was she now hated him.

The Search

As soon as she could walk without cringing at the pain, Susan headed back to the town, to the cafe. Cassandra rushed over to help fit the double pram through the doors, trying to work out where she'd seen the new mother before.

"They're so beautiful. What are they called?"

"Coffee?" Glenys asked.

"Tap water please."

"Coffee's on the house. It's tiring having little ones."

"Water."

Cassandra tried to place the customer as she manoeuvred the pram next to a booth. The lady didn't look as exhausted as Mary Macintyre when she'd had her twins. Mary always cried saying, "What have I done? What's happened to me? I didn't think it would be like this."

One of the babies whimpered.

"Shush." Susan nudged the wheel of the pram. The child stopped crying.

Cassandra re-filled Michael Moon's coffee cup. He ordered gooseberry pie with double cream even though his cholesterol was high and the doctor had said he needed to forgo eating quite so very much now.

"It must be hard work having the two," said Cassandra. "But double the pleasure."

"Not really."

"My sister had one and another a year later, an accident. She was exhausted all the time. I took a week off to help out and even with me and her husband at home we'd all be on our knees each evening." She was glad she'd done it though. It helped confirm that it wasn't the path she wanted to take. Not yet. She'd go travelling first. There were so many cities to explore, so many countries. "Do they wake much? I guess they do being so little."

"They sleep through," said Susan, with a hint of pride.

"No? That's amazing. How old are they?"

"Eight weeks."

"Eight weeks! Glenys, did you hear that? Eight weeks and they're sleeping through."

"You should sell that secret," called out Michael. "None of mine did that until they were nearly two."

"My sister's youngest still creeps into their bed most nights."

"Aw, no harm in that, whatever you need to get some shut eye."

To Susan it was about control, teaching them who was in charge. She was the alpha female. Moon man was sweating profusely. It wasn't hot enough to warrant that. He rolled his left shoulder round and round, undid the second button on his shirt even though his collar was already loose.

"You should go to the hospital."

"What?" he laughed, massaging his chest.

Cassandra scooped extra ice-cream around the edge of the gooseberry pie plate and made a twirly pattern with the spray cream right up to the pastry, just how he liked it.

"You need to see a doctor."

He looked at Susan like she was mad. She held his stare. Fear came. Glenys got ready to intervene.

"You're overweight, a smoker, sweating, feeling a tightness on your left hand side. All the signs of a heart about to crash."

Glenys and Cassandra stared at Michael.

"It's hot in here with the sun and all the glass."

But now he noticed none of them were sweating. He groaned in response to a sudden, excruciating pain.

"I'll drive," said Glenys. "Cassie, you okay here?" she looked pointedly at the back of Susan's head.

"Sure." Cassandra opened the door for them. "You go. Hurry. And I'm sure you'll be fine Michael." When she shut the door she shivered. Cassandra was in awe of medical knowledge. She'd picked up an anatomy book in the second hand shop and marvelled at how medical people remembered all those facts. "Are you a doctor?"

"A nurse."

"You saved his life. That's incredible." To go home and tell your boyfriend you'd saved an actual life that day, there couldn't be a better feeling. "Who's got a clever mummy?" She cooed at the babies.

"She likes you. She hasn't smiled before. Does the boy from the morgue still come here?"

Cassandra clapped her hands together.

"You're the watch lady aren't you? I thought I knew you from somewhere. You brought Calton back his watch. He was so relieved. It—"

"I've not seen him in a while."

"He moved away."

Susan regained her composure so quickly Cassandra noticed nothing.

"Yes. The thing is, I lost the forwarding address he gave me and I promised to write and he must think I'm so rude that I forgot. As you can see I've been a bit busy."

"Yeah," Cassandra said, kneeling in front of the pram. "They're so gorgeous."

Susan tried to get through to the dense head below her.

"My husband knew him. They were great friends. Did he mention which town he was moving to? I've got double baby brain and can't remember. Was it a T it began with or a W?"

"I've no idea."

"Not even a guess?"

"He had a big meal, said it was his on the road blow out, dessert as well as a main which he'd never ordered before." She kept stroking the babies. "He was a bit mysterious wasn't he? But kind of cool. Jenny Taggert used to come in whenever she saw him through the window. She had such a crush on him. I didn't get it. He had nice eyes I guess but not my type. And too young."

Susan stood up and steered the pram towards the door. A back wheel got caught on the corner of the counter and instead of cajoling it round she repeatedly banged the pram against the side as if it would crumble and fall out of her way. Flakes of white paint fell on the floor.

"Here, let me help you."

Cassandra bent down to lift the wheel. Susan moved the pram too quickly so Cassandra's fingers got caught and cut.

"Ouch." She sucked up the blood. "Don't worry. No problem. Doesn't hurt."

Cassandra squeezed past the pram to open the door and Susan felt like ramming it into the wall or pushing it out onto the road. Let it run in front of whatever came, let fate take them from her. Baby two cried all the way down the street.

"Shut up," said Susan. "Just shut the hell up would you."

~

Susan was in the sort of mood where she could go up against four in a fight and beat the lot of them because her anger gave her super-human strength and I'm not scared of you so don't dare mess with me powers. Not wanting to go to prison for harming the defenceless ones, she left the babies awake in their shared cot and went into the kitchen where she picked the largest pan out of the cupboard and threw it on the floor so hard it bounced twice. When she picked it up the metal was dented. Not enough. She raised the arm that was holding it and bashed the pan against the fridge door, two pieces of metal dented now, one white with hints of grey in the centre of the crater its attacker had disfigured it with. Susan contained her urge to scream as she whacked the pan into the door a second time. Too loud. There must be no human noise as then the neighbours would hear and the nosy bastards would come knockety knocking, checking she was alright, were the children hurt, such tiny darlings. Susan needed no-one in her life but herself and her two children. Not even the children. She didn't need them. She'd leave them if a part of her wasn't tied to them by a reason she couldn't fathom, though it was important she got the anger out without hurting them as otherwise there'd be all sorts of trouble. Neighbours would call the police who'd ring the doorbell.

Her past would be poked into. Fools would infuriate her, an anger she'd have to hide behind smiles and I'm fines every five minutes. She wasn't sure she had the pretence in her, not today, not at this hour, not like she was able to last week. Maybe the next week would be better. A scream escaped as she pounded the pan onto the sofa not wanting to damage any more of her apartment, not wanting the damage she did to cost her money that she'd worked so hard to gather.

The cushions were less satisfying. They dented but weren't hurt, not like she wanted them to be. She whacked them repeatedly, wishing the covers would tear like skin, almost ashamed at imagining they were her babies while feeling proud that she wasn't actually injuring them. Look at the control within her, not many mothers were as strong when the anger got hold of them, so self-aware, so full of discipline.

The girls cried. How she hated their noise, the way it went right into her head like a catheter deep into a bladder. A pox and a piss on them. She ran to the bedroom.

"Shut up. Shut up you god-damn freakoids. Shut your mouths! Let me be why don't you. I hate you so much. I wish I'd never had you. Shut up shut up shut up." She whacked the edge of the cot so hard it wobbled off two legs. The side of the cot hit the wall before tipping back until it rested on four corners again. Rather than crying louder both babies went quiet, eyes to the ceiling. One of them nearly got a thumb in its mouth, legs involuntarily kicking but even then looking as if she was trying not to disturb her mother.

Susan knew that feeling. She sank to the floor as she recognised what she'd turned into.

252

Mrs Roth squinted. The contrast between the darkness in the hall and light on the porch was too sharp. She blinked at the silhouette which looked like a lady with some sort of shopping trolley behind her.

"Sorry, I've nothing to donate."

"I'm here to see Calton, from the morgue."

"I'm afraid he's not here."

"I can wait."

"He doesn't lodge here anymore."

"Oh. I must have got my dates muddled. I could have sworn it was next week he was leaving."

"No. Sorry. Not at all. He's not been here for months now."

Mrs Roth got nothing in return for her smile. A baby cried. No. Two babies. The lady ignored them.

"Did he leave a forwarding address?"

"What's that behind you?"

"It doesn't matter."

"Of course it matters. Move to the side." She poked her head around Susan's chest. "Well aren't they just adorable."

Susan stared at her daughters. She still hadn't experienced the whoosh of love, only the whoosh of resentment. She took them for a daily walk to stop herself from squeezing them too hard. Every day she was tempted to leave the pram down a side street, go to her rented room, pack a bag, get on a bus. But they'd trace her. Of course they would. As the mother, she couldn't escape. Not like her husband, not like her afternoon stand did.

"Are you alright darling?"

The kindness in the old lady's voice took Susan by surprise. Most people shared a look with the person next to them. She heard their judgmental whispers: bad mother, cold and callous, hard and unloving. One even said bitch as she'd passed her.

"That's a nice way to talk in front of your children," Susan had shouted back.

She wished the lady had stopped so she could fight her. She was angry enough, had felt nothing but anger since giving birth. Maybe a fight would get it out of her system. Or maybe she'd end up knocking someone unconscious and go straight to jail. She thought mothers were meant to stand together, all those superficial smiles to strangers in ante-natal waiting rooms. But now the babies were out no-one asked how are you today, until this landlady.

Mrs Roth sensed the girl was a new mother who was on the brink.

"Why don't you come inside? I've fresh orange juice in the fridge."

"I'm a widow," said Susan, all matter of fact.

Mrs Roth nodded. "It's terribly hard. You must still be in shock."

"Did Calton leave his forwarding address?"

"No."

"Would you mind if I looked in his room? I leant him a book."

"I cleaned it out. There was nothing left. And there's been a different tenant since he was here."

"Perhaps I could double check?"

Mrs Roth noticed the mark on the girl's hand where a wedding ring had sat so surely Cal couldn't be the father. He was too young, too stoned, too flaky.

"Of course. I'll keep an eye on the little ones."

There was a muslin bag full of lavender sitting on the pillow in Cal's old room. Susan picked it up and sniffed deeply. Nothing. Not since the hurt to the back of her head from the brick wall John had shoved her against.

She sat on the bed where Cal used to sleep and ran her hands over the white pillowcase. A navy blue eiderdown was tucked tightly under the mattress, all ready for a new guest. The sink was sludge free. The pale grey walls had been scrubbed with sugar soap and the blind was half way down. She pulled it up and opened the window, looking for the spot she used to watch him from. He can't have known how she spied, that she knew he smoked drugs. With her back to the wall by the side of the house she'd seen the smoke that was thicker than cigarettes and found two butts that were filled with greenery as well as tobacco. If he was still there she could have blackmailed him for company or punished him by telling the police about his illegal habit.

~

Mrs Roth was holding the largest baby in the crook of her right arm.

"What's her name?"

They looked like a granny and granddaughter. If Mrs Roth had been her mother maybe Susan would have enjoyed childhood. She saw a bag on the floor, Luella's yarns.

"Luella."

"I adore that name. It suits you doesn't it darling?" Mrs Roth kissed the baby's head. It gurgled, confused, got another kiss. "Cheek to cheek, that's what I love. So soft, it always amazes me and the beautiful smell of them." She breathed in Luella's scent. "Gorgeous. The other one's the sleeper?"

"More alert when she's awake."

"Ah, clever then."

Mrs Roth put Luella over her shoulder and sniffed her downy hair. The pressure on her twisted knuckles aggravated the arthritis but it was worth the pain to feel the smooth skin and smell the innocence. Susan pretended to give all her attention to the other one. She looked at her, stroked her cheek, felt an obvious phoney so stopped.

"He was a lovely boy. Quiet but well brought up. You can tell can't you? How did you meet him?"

"At work."

"In the morgue?"

"I need to go. It's near their bed time."

"He said he wanted to be back by the water. I think he grew up near the sea. He mentioned walking by the water, missing the smell of it and the mountains. Perhaps he meant a lake rather than the sea. It was like he wanted to be there again."

Susan pushed the pram down the hallway.

"He got a bus at around nine o'clock, if that helps. Say hello when you find him. Say hello from Mrs Roth and tell him I miss him."

Once the front door was shut Susan kicked the wheel of the pram twice with her foot.

"Pah," she grunted, kicking the pram a third time, so hard it shunted forwards. The front wheels started to tumble down the steps meaning she had to reach out and grab it.

~

Susan fumed. Look at him not taking responsibility for what he'd done, him and the other but the first one was dead so there was nothing she could do about that. It made her blood boil. How dare the morgue boy not be there to pick up baby number two, all weak, listless, fragile. If Susan knew where he was she'd leave the baby on his doorstep, knock and run away, see how he liked that. Though if she did, she'd be lambasted, of course she would. Whatever town, hamlet, city he lived in, the neighbours and landlady would take pity on him, help him raise it, call her a demented evil slut for abandoning a child. Yet he could get away with it. Folks would laugh or roll their eyes as if what else do you expect, he's a man, boys will be boys, that's what they do darling. That's the way it had happened throughout history. Not good enough.

~

The lady at the bus station told Susan the buses that left between nine and nine thirty headed East. She bought a map in the bookstore, opened it up and searched for a town near a lake. One stood out, near a huge lake that would take at least an hour to walk around. There was an H for hospital sign. She could earn a living there.

Calton

Calton travelled West, stopped to earn money, travelled further West, stopped to earn more money, and so on and onwards until he reached the remotest city in the country. He found a job at the Botanic Gardens. It was where he belonged, outside, nurturing the land rather than stuck with dead bodies underneath it.

The guilt of lying to Mrs Roth about the direction he'd taken sat lightly on his chest. He was sure it was the best decision for both him and her. The widow was unbalanced, full of a grim sadness and he didn't want Mrs Roth having to fight that, not at her age. Plus it was for the widow's good. Cal did not want to be with her.

~

The sea smelt different to Byron, the mint choc chip ice cream wasn't as flavoursome but the weed, that was powerful stuff. In his most stoned moments Cal planned a route home, pictured Johnny, Ann and Mrs Irving greeting him. Sometimes they smiled, sometimes they were frowning. Would they remember him five years from now or in fifteen? Not that it mattered. He was fine by himself. As long as he had a smoke, he needed no-one.

Susan

After making a beeline for the back of the bus, Susan lay the babies on either side of her then wedged the cases between them and the seats in front so they couldn't roll off. She chose the night bus to save on accommodation costs. Other passengers spotted them so sat as near to the front as they could. They even chose to sit next to a stranger rather than risk being close to a crying child. But there was no need. The babies merely gurgled occasionally.

Susan remembered Mrs Roth holding Luella. She, the mother, still didn't want to pick up her children unless it was to move one from A to B. There was something wrong with her, there had to be. Was her lack of feeling today, all of the days, the result of the knock to the head, the big one when the doctor visited because she didn't wake up after the smelling salts? Did the latest big knock mean the chance of her liking her children was utterly lost along with her ability to smell and the use of her taste buds? She scrunched her eyes closed. It was too complicated and too upsetting to think life might have been different if she hadn't hit the fire-place and the ground so hard. She was who she was and that was the end of it. She squashed her bag behind her lower back and swallowed a pink pill followed by an orange one.

~

The driver didn't touch her. You never knew if they were a bit crazy or not. One time he woke a teenage girl and she'd hit him hard enough to bruise his cheek, before running off the bus.

"Hello. Hello, we're here."

He smiled at the babies. They were awake but quiet. Susan opened her eyes. He was a different driver to the one who'd started the journey.

"Ma'am, we're here," he said.

She checked behind him. The coach was empty. To her right she spied the pram on the pavement and her cases that had been placed beside it. Susan stood up and stretched. Without asking her permission, the driver picked up the nameless one who was sucking her thumb.

"Come on little darling."

Susan picked up Luella and followed him off the coach.

"I've never seen a baby so well behaved. You're a quiet one aren't you? My wife and I are trying. Soon hopefully, eh baba? What are their names? Are they identical?"

"Luella. And your one's Lara."

A girl in her school had been called Lara. She had long hair all the way down her back. Her mother styled it every morning: French plaits, normal plaits, high bunches, pretty clips. Susan always envied hair like that and grew hers past her shoulders as soon as she left home.

"Lara and Luella. Aren't they the most precious sweethearts."

Susan squeezed the smaller case into the basket under the pram seat and pulled the other one behind her.

"Shall I find you a taxi?"

"No need. It's not far."

"Are you sure? Your hands look pretty full with the both of them. Is someone meeting you?"

The word pah caught in Susan's mouth making her cough. Her throat was sore as if there was a lump in it. She unwrapped a lozenge and sucked.

The bus driver watched her walk away as if she was sure of where she was going. After two left turns, once Susan was out of sight, she stopped. A blue car drove past her. There were no other pedestrians. An H for Hospital sign pointed down the street. Opposite was a bank and on the other corner a store that doubled as a post office. Three doors down from that a bell rang as a man walked out of a cafe. Her stomach rumbled.

"Food followed by an apartment followed by your father."

"Ugh," went Luella. Lara was too busy sucking her thumb to make a noise.

"Shush," grunted the mother. Luella started to cry. Susan's chest ached as well as her throat. She closed her eyes and pretended she couldn't hear the baby.

What she couldn't hear wouldn't bother her.

What she couldn't see wouldn't bother her.

What she couldn't taste wouldn't bother her.

What she couldn't smell wouldn't bother her.

And to not be bothered, that was wise. To feel nothing meant she would survive where others didn't. It meant she was the champion.

Susan kicked up the brake on the pram much harder than she needed to, jolting the girls. She crossed the road.

"Food followed by an apartment followed by a job."

Luella gurgled. Her mother looked at her but felt no love. "Onwards."

Acknowledgements

A big thank you to my husband and girls for your support as I write, especially when you cook the dinner.

Huge thanks to my wonderful cover designer Jennie, to Leigh for typesetting the book so brilliantly, and to Sue for the proof reading. When a manuscript is forwarded to you all, I know it's in great hands.

Thank you to Sue and Jo for your feedback on the full manuscript – time is precious, your advice and enthusiasm are so appreciated. For the laughs and encouragement, thanks to: Sue, Emma, Katie, Paul H, Paul E, Victoria, Dom, Pippa, Alex, Sophie, and Hannah.

I'd also like to thank my Twitter book friends and all the lovely book bloggers for your hard work and reviews, especially Rónán Hession, Jules Swain, James Endeacott and Pete Keeley. You won't realise it but your positivity gave me a huge boost when I was editing *PAH*. It's been great to virtually meet you.

Also, by Orla Owen
The Lost Thumb

'What a find. Pacey and intense (I galloped through
the last 160 pages today)... I had to stay and sit at
Victoria station until I finished it.'
Rónán Hession

'I don't want this to end – such a great read –
thanks for the words... a triumph.'
James Endeacott

LARA AND LUELLA JEFFREYS lead
isolated lives until the night they
are left alone for the first time, and
Luella decides to have some fun.
That evening goes horribly wrong.
After Luella wakes up in hospital,
she's kept prisoner at home with
her mother acting as her warden.
Lara is sent to school to keep up the
pretence that she is fine, her sister
is fine, and the world is fine. Except

they aren't. The local storekeeper, sensing that something's
wrong, pushes her son to befriend Lara but the results of
her meddling are deadly...

For more information on Orla Owen and her books visit
her website www.orlaowen.com or follow her on Twitter
@orlaowenwriting